I WILL SURVIVE

GO THERE.

OTHER TITLES AVAILABLE FROM PUSH

I WILL SURVIVE
KRISTEN KEMP

PUSH

SCHOLASTIC INC.

NEW YORK   TORONTO   LONDON   AUCKLAND   SYDNEY

MEXICO CITY   NEW DELHI   HONG KONG   BUENOS AIRES

ISBN 0-439-12195-7

12 11 10 9 8 7 6 5 4 3 2 1   2 3 4 5 6 7/0

Printed in the U.S.A.   40
First Scholastic/PUSH printing, June 2002

To Kelly Estep, my teenage partner in mischief and mayhem

I WILL SURVIVE

CHAPTER ONE

There was a long silence in the car, which was unusual anytime Melisha was around. Of course, she was the first to break it, right as she and Jack turned onto her street.

"God, I'm a little sore. Probably played too much Ping-Pong."

"Yeah, Ping-Pong will wear you out, Melisha. Especially when you have such stiff competition — like me," Jack said.

"You know you only win when I let you win. Isn't it about time that you start getting over your soggy self, anyway?" she replied before she began humming a nerve-rattling show tune.

"If I'm so pathetic why do you —"

"Ooomps, I'm sooo sorry to cut you off, but here we are — my house! Lemme out!"

"My pleasure."

Jack threw his shiny black VW Beetle into reverse. He looked at Melisha, and his mind started spinning faster than his new retro set of wheels. He had a fleeting thought that despite her subtle trashiness, there was something magical about Melisha. Maybe it was the dramatic way she tossed her curly auburn hair, teasing him with shots of her tanned neck. Or maybe there was something much more simple about her. After all, she possessed a handful of carefully crafted, boy-bewitching habits. For example, she would strategically show off glimpses of her leopard panties while resting her feet on the dashboard of the Beetle. But life was such a cheesy made-for-TV movie to Melisha — her soap-opera antics did get old sometimes. Jack thought of himself as more of a too-cool-for-school groovy guy — slick, smooth, and self-confident.

Melisha interrupted Jack's thoughts as he skidded beside the curb. "You know you'll miss me, honey-Ping-Pong-pie," she cooed. "Call me later. Oh, and tell Ellen toodles for me."

With that, she bounced through the door of her tacky pink house.

Jack kept wondering what it was about her. He decided Melisha must have some sort of voodoo love spell over him. Plus, they always played a good game of Ping-Pong.

His thoughts wandered to the next order of business on his agenda. Ellen.

Ellen was sitting on her bed, listening to her Barenaked Ladies CD and trying to snap out of it. As usual, she was just trying to score some alone-time in silence after another stressful school day. But there was no chance of that happening. Getting out of a funk would be especially hard because of the whining going on downstairs. Her sister, Eve, had a loud shrill voice that could pierce extra earring holes in a girl's ears — and she was sure using it. She was going on and on about the way her butt looked in her Miss Corncob competition bathing suit, and how it was going to ruin her chances at the local beauty pageant in two weeks.

"It's so flat!" Ellen heard her scream. Ellen listened to her sister's I'm-a-bone body complaints all the time. Meanwhile, Ellen was worried that her butt would expand three sizes and blow up before Jack's party tomorrow night. Ugh. It was bad enough being the not-as-gorgeous older sister. But having a sibling who was only nine months younger and looked like a *Cosmo* model (only prettier) made Ellen contemplate the life of an orphan runaway. Everyone loved bright and cheery Eve. Their parents considered her the family's precious little gem. But to Ellen, Eve was pure cubic zirconia. Really. She was as fake as their mom's blond hair. And when Eve whined again, "But it's *so* small, Mom. And my *chest*?! Did you see Drewcilla Locklear's *curves*?" Ellen thought about yelling out: "If only your zits were as low profile as your ass —" She decided to refrain from retaliation though; that would be stooping to Eve's level — something Ellen did not want to do.

So she kept her thoughts to herself. At least she had an easy-breezy maintenance-free complexion — not to mention a solid set of size C's. And if it wasn't for her funky, foul mood, she would have felt bad for thinking such bitchy thoughts.

Commotion ensued downstairs as their mom tried to calm Eve down and a spat began. Yep, *now* Ellen was out of her funk. The havoc was humorous. It wasn't like Ellen was truly evil or anything. Her sister just brought out the mean streak in her.

As expected, Ellen soon heard her can't-we-all-just-get-along mom coming up the stairs to cool off. Then the doorbell rang.

She could hear her mom's footsteps trail back down, and then the sound of her boyfriend's voice. *Hallelujah*. Jack was buttering up her mom — and Eve was flirting with him, the little opportunistic parasite. Ellen took a quick look in her mirror, but for no reason really. She expected it to crack and fall off the wall in disgust because it had no choice but to look back at her. The black tank tops she wore complemented her caramel eyes and shiny black hair that she hated. Sure she had a pug nose and a few freckles, but she was far from the daggiest girl in the eleventh grade, even if she looked nothing like the hair-dryer-brained Miss Teenage Thang she had for a sister.

The bedroom door opened.

"Hey."

"Hey," Jack said as he hugged her, "accidentally" close against Ellen's set of C's.

How sweet, Ellen thought. Jack had been extra moody lately so it was nice to see him glowing and affectionate. Ellen, who had friends but didn't hang out with the homecoming-queen crowd, always considered herself lucky — wait, make that blessed — to have landed Jack. He was a filet mignon among the chopped sirloin of their junior class. He was classy, smart, and totally Banana Republic in an Indiana town where everyone else shopped at Wal-Mart. He was almost six feet tall, with gorgeous golden skin. Plus, his all-that aura was so sexy. And Jack was all hers, despite the jealousy of the entire cheer-leading squad. They'd been together four months — an eternity for sixteen-year-old Ellen — and they were in love.

Or at least Ellen was.

"Wanna do it?" Jack asked in his usual, playfully serious manner.

"Nice to see you, too," she answered, irritated. She didn't say anything else — but she wanted Jack to know she could not be played. So when he tried to hug her again, she forced herself to nudge him away.

He smiled at her and somehow gave her a wink without really winking. Maybe it was just the way his eyes twinkled.

Despite herself, she thought: *Isn't he just A.1. sauce? No, better, he's my tangy zest of Miracle Whip.*

"I heard your sister again — you left your window open. Have you been sneaking those nasty Capris in here? It's bad enough that your dad smokes in this house."

"No." Ellen fibbed. "Why does everyone worship her?"

"Everyone? Not me. I only worship you."

"Well, then, take me to your palace."

Jack did live in a three-bedroom palace, in the fanciest neighborhood in all of Shitville, Indiana. He and his dad, Rich, always had nice cars and the coolest clothes. But they didn't have Jack's mom — she left a long time ago. Jack never talked about it, so Ellen never asked. Neither did his dad, who was known around town as sexy, brilliant, sexy, talkative, friendly, and sexy. He gave Ellen and Jack lots of privacy and handed out twenties frequently. Ellen was convinced that Jack's house was heaven. There was even a freezer full of Phish Food — just for Ellen.

The sitcom-cute couple sat on the back swing for an hour, just talking and giggling. Then they started making out — you could do that there. Jack's dad didn't care. Ellen's mind was filled with *Mmms* and *Ahhhs* and spoonfuls of luscious, creamy Ben & Jerry's.

"Wanna play some Ping-Pong, Ellen?" Jack whispered in her ear as his hand undid the buttons of her new Gap cargo pants.

"God, Jack! You know I'm not ready to have sex with you

5

yet!" *Why does he always have to call it goofy names like "Ping-Pong" anyway?* "You're so annoying," she said.

"What is?" Jack asked.

"Let's just forget about it, okay?" Ellen said.

He was peeved, but he finally let it slide, and she was happy. Oh, was she happy.

CHAPTER TWO

Ellen walked into her house feeling pretty great about her killer boyfriend. She could live in her own mind forever just thinking about him. She went into the kitchen to grab a post-make-out Creamsicle. She wanted to savor it in silence. That way, she could make her too-few moments with Jack linger. She could focus on how it felt to be alone with him. *Ahhh.* Things were perfect.

Then her solitude was so rudely interrupted. Her sister swept by as if the universe couldn't exist without her presence in it. She was flailing her arms around, practicing some dumb performance for the beauty pageant. One of these spasms thwacked Ellen right in the nose. Ellen wanted to smack her back and might have done it if Eve hadn't hightailed it out of her way.

"Bye, Mommy and Daddy! If you need to reach me, just call Sara's!" Eve yelled as she left to go to her best friend's house for the night. Without asking, she took off in their Tempo, the one she and Ellen "shared." Ellen tried to trip her on the way out but missed. Eve stuck out her tongue, and Ellen felt lame.

"Ellen, honey, will you answer the phone if it rings? And tell them we're busy," her mom, just-call-me-Heather, yelled to her from the living room. Ellen could hear her parents fiddling with the VCR. When she looked in on them, Jane Fonda was on the TV screen talking about how much better life could be when you relied on yoga. Her mom was in a red leotard from the 1970s (which — damn — she looked great in) and her dad had on little blue jogging shorts with a white stripe down each side. He was wearing worn-out dress socks with holes in the toes. He didn't even have his shirt on. Ellen almost choked on her Creamsicle. *Aren't there laws against these things?*

Ellen was sorta close to her mom — they were a lot alike, most of the time. When Ellen was younger, Heather constantly reminded her not to feel crappy about her sister's astonishing looks, but to be proud of her own, um, *intellectual talents* instead. Like Heather, Ellen was spunky, and she was into writing. In college, Heather had won some national poetry contest sponsored by the *New Yorker* magazine. But she gave it up when she married her college English professor, Ellen's dad (Ed), and started helping him research/write his textbooks and papers.

At her mom's insistence, Ellen always kept a journal, wrote short stories and poems, and actually got A's in her English classes. Anyway, Ellen's talents usually made her literary parents pee with pride. And since Eve was bound to be prancing around on an MTV video one day, Ellen had to impress everybody somehow. She set her sights on getting into Columbia's or even Harvard's writing program. Admission to either one was reserved for only the most clever, devoted writers — kinda like if you were chosen to go backstage at one of your favorite band's concerts. What made Ellen happier than anything was that Eve

8

would not be caught dead on any of those campuses. She wanted to go to Indiana University (only because she thought basketball players were hot). But getting in anywhere would be tough for Eve. After all, the girl could barely spell *XOXO*.

Ellen headed toward her room. Before Jane Fonda turned her house into a New Age commune via VCR, Ellen was hoping to ask her mom for some good guy advice. But obviously that would be impossible. Her calm, cool parents were going organic on her. Ever since her dad turned fifty a month ago, he'd been in a midlife crisis. He switched to low-tar cigarettes, exercised at six A.M., wore clothes from Abercrombie, and traded in his Explorer for a Honda Del Sol. He even grew a scary Grateful Dead beard for a while, until Heather refused to be seen in public with him. Heather herself, a forty-year-old mother, was also having some trouble facing the reality of aging. In addition to yoga, she'd taken up meditation, herbal remedies, and extra-firm tofu. They all sucked. Ellen peeked into the living room again and found her parents in the elephant position, giggling like high-school sweethearts.

Who are these people in my parents' house? Ellen wondered. *What would it take to have my normal, Bud-drinking parents back?!* She had heard enough of all that yoga crap at school recently because her crunchy English teacher, Mr. Cruz, was way into it, too. So until E.T. returned her real parents home, Ellen decided to retreat to her room. She opened the window, lit a Capri Ultra Light, and called her best friend Melisha.

"I need to talk," Ellen said.

"Right now, sweetie tweetie? I can't — I'm in the middle of costume design. We're doing *Romeo and Juliet* for the next school play, and I've got six people here helping me think out

9

my wardrobe possibilities. I swear, I'm gonna look just as smashing as that dog-eyed Claire Danes wench. If you want to come to our after-school practices, you'd make a *great* stage-hand. Gotta go, ta-ta! I cross my heart I'll call you later."

"Whatever," Ellen said, and plunked down the phone. She felt totally blown off.

Melisha's mom, Di, had been best friends with Ellen's mom for twenty years. So it was easy for Ellen and Melisha to be best friends, too. But lately, Melisha had been way too preoccupied with her new position as president of the drama club. Ellen was happy for Melisha, but also lonely without her. Ellen had no desire to be a drama queen. Come to think of it, she and Melisha had less and less in common. Except gossip — boy, did they have a good time last year when the girl playing Little Orphan Annie started getting it on with Daddy Warbucks. But they'd been together so long that they seemed stuck with each other. At least Ellen and Melisha usually had great conversations — especially about sex.

Next on the speed dial was Julian, Ellen's other best friend. Julian was a sweet guy who had an even sweeter crush on Ellen. She kind of knew but chose to blow it off because she just wanted to be friends. Messing up their friendship would be as ill fated as drinking a hot Diet Coke. See, Ellen and Julian were soul mates. They both listened to the same music; they both loved writing; they were coeditors of the school paper; and they had the exact same taste in movies. Ellen always thought Julian would turn out to be gay. Finding a straight guy this sensitive and insightful was damn near impossible.

"Are you otherwise preoccupied, Julian?" Ellen asked with an un-Ellen-like tinge of desperation.

"With what? Of course not, Ellen. I'm never too busy for you," he said, melting at the sexy scratchiness of her nicotine-charred voice.

"Wanna come over? I'm in hell over this whole Jack thing. He wants to do it soon. I think I'm gonna, but I really need to talk to you about it."

"Oh, that. You know what I have to say." Julian thought of the rumor he'd just heard about Jack and Melisha. He'd spent the whole day hoping it was true, and that he'd get to tell Ellen soon. "You know I can't stand him. He's so stuck-up and arrogant." Julian paused before he added, "I think he's using you, Elle." He loved to call her Elle — it sounded so sophisticated and glamorous.

"*Sooo* not true. Just today he got this sweet look on his face and told me he really loved me."

Silence. Julian was brokenhearted — he fought back the lump rising up in his throat.

"Julian?"

"Well, I'll come over, but I don't wanna talk about Jack anymore. We'll just get in a catfight if we do."

"Whatever, just keep me company. Bring a movie, will ya?"

"Yeah, Elle. I'll bring *Thelma and Louise* and some Phish Food. Sound good?"

"Now I know why I love you," Ellen said, thinking about what a girl Julian really was, and how happy she had always been about that.

Julian only wished that she really loved him. To him, Ellen was air, shelter, and nourishment. She was as much a part of him as the white stuff is to an Oreo. Enthusiastically, Julian got ready to head out.

While he was on his way, Ellen popped out her diary and sprayed Glade all over her rock-band-covered room.

Sex him.

Sex him not.

Sex him.

Sex him not.

Uggggh.

Should I really lose my virginity to Jack? It's so sacred — I mean it's like choosing a college. You have to choose the right one or you'll spend the rest of your life regretting the entire experience.

And it can ruin your future. What if I go through with it and turn into a psycho slut — I'm talkin' Single White Female *on Capri Ultra Lights.*

So what happens if I wait? I'll just end up losing it to someone else later, right? Someone not as beautiful . . . someone I'm not in love with.

I know what I want to do.

I want to take a chance for once in my life.

I want to sex Jack.

CHAPTER THREE

Julian stopped at Blockbuster, then Ben & Jerry's. He was determined to brighten Ellen's mood and make her forget that evil dick, Jack. Julian hated him. If there was ever a guy to be jealous of, it was Jack. Julian didn't look anything like Josh Hartnett (Jack did); he didn't have a spanking-new Beetle (he had a rusty Camry); and Ellen *was not* freaking out about sexing Julian (well, in his dreams she was). And Julian certainly didn't have an obnoxious four-porch palace or a cool dad who left for long weekends so you could have wild parties in the house.

Julian was just different, but not a total tool or anything. He had friends — Ellen and Melisha and some other girls. A long time ago, he discovered that he got along better with the female brand of the human species. The guys he hung out with always wanted to play cards, set bugs on fire, and then watch football. Pure torture. With boys named Bruce, Bump, and, well, Jack, Julian couldn't exactly yap for an hour on the phone, go shopping, and then watch *Real World* marathons while pigging out on peanut butter M&M's. To say that Julian had more in common with girls was to say that, yes, chocolate truffles must be washed down with cold milk. Girls were always understanding about Julian's downfalls — awful allergies and his nose-spray medications. When he whipped out his inhaler, most boys just called him a daisy-loving dork.

It got old, though. If you're friends with all the girls, it's kinda hard to go out with them. Especially Ellen. If Julian could have snapped his fingers and made her *like him* like him, he would have worn out his fingertips trying. But, all things considered, hanging out with Ellen was almost good enough. Or at least it used to be. Lately, his passion for her was causing him to lose patience. He didn't know how much longer he could take the torture of being near Ellen without being able to touch her the way he longed to. Tonight he hoped he'd finally get his chance. Julian planned to tell his Elle that he was *crazy* about her. But after he let her in on the nasty little rumor he'd heard.

Julian had his whole speech planned by the time he pulled into Ellen's driveway. Unfortunately, Melisha's car was parked there, too.

Damn. Disappointed isn't the word to describe how Julian felt. But for him, it was all too familiar. He saw the two of them sneaking cigarettes out of Ellen's upstairs window — they looked ridiculous with those Capri Ultra Lights hanging out of their mouths. When Julian rang the doorbell, Heather answered it, and he went upstairs.

"Elle, why's your mom in a red leotard?" Julian asked without his usual cheerfulness.

"No clue."

"I brought you two *Thelma and Lou* —" Julian said before choking on the Glade-covered cigarette stench in the room.

The two girls didn't even notice that their antics affected his allergies — they were knee-deep into their conversation.

"He acted so, um, so *wounded*, Mel. And all I did was *not* have sex with him," Ellen said.

"Jerk," Melisha replied.

"I think he was really hurt, though. I've told him that I will, and I really will. I just don't feel it yet — well, I *feel* it but I don't *feel* it. Do you know what I mean?"

Julian just stood there, listening and truth-staring Melisha. He decided to be silent on this one.

"Ohmigod, I know what you mean. Honey, you know what I went through with my ex, Max. He was dying for sex. We did everything but. And just when I was ready to give it up, he dumped me."

"Not a good story, Mel," Ellen said. "I was kinda hoping for some *helpful* advice. "

"Just wait, that's all. You can never know when he'll break up with you."

"What the hell kinda thing is that to say? Remind me to call you next time I try to commit suicide."

"Sorry, I just think you should wait."

"Well, I'm not gonna. I've made up my mind."

"You'll be sorry. I don't want to see you get hurt, that's all." Melisha was getting very uncomfortable with the whole conversation, and Julian noticed when she started to fidget. Ellen didn't notice anything. She was hallucinating in Jack Land.

Finally, Julian piped up. "Can't we just watch the movie?"

Melisha went home right after Thelma and Louise hurled themselves off that killer cliff. Since Melisha had been complaining about her Saturday morning drama club meetings, Ellen was glad she left. As usual, though, Melisha forgot her leopard-print jacket. She rushed back in to get it, pulled a piece of gum out of her pocket, then left.

Ellen started to feel cranky.

Finally alone with Ellen, Julian wanted to make The Move. His stomach felt like it had four cups of coffee in it, though, and his allergies started to attack. He pulled out his inhaler and collected himself. After a deep breath, he told Ellen, "There's something I have to say."

"What, Julian?" Ellen was kinda hoping Julian would go home soon, too. Usually, she wanted him to stay, but right now she was exhausted.

"You won't believe what I heard today. You won't believe it, Elle," Julian said, trying to be gentle.

"I'll believe it."

"Well, you know how my little brother plays with Jack's next-door neighbor?"

"Yeah." Ellen was so sick of Julian acting like he knew everything about Jack because of his geeky brother. It was annoying. Ellen suspected that Julian was just jade-green jealous. And she was too tired (and grumpy) to be her normal, sensitive self. It was awkward enough when Julian brought the subject of Jack up. And Ellen was already feeling fussy. Not a good combination.

"He said that he saw Jack kissing a girl today."

"So what? I was over there all day, he must've seen us. He's just being a sick little perve."

"Elle, my brother told me that the girl wasn't you. He's sure of it."

"Your brother's brain-dead, Julian. You know he doesn't like me very much."

"He likes you just fine," Julian lied — his younger brother actually hated Ellen. She scared him. "Anyway, he said that she had auburn hair and a little pink sweater."

At this point, Ellen wasn't listening.

"Ellen," Julian continued, "I'm pretty sure it was Melisha today. I am *sure* of it."

Now Ellen was listening. She couldn't believe this crap oozing out of Julian's mouth. "What the hell is wrong with you, Julian?" Ellen was on the verge of snapping and her words were about to get acidic. She tried to hold them back. But she was angry, and she couldn't. The day had been full of drama. She didn't need any of Julian's.

He was surprised at her bitchiness. "I . . . just . . . thought . . . you, um, had a right to know."

"You're so full of shit. I know you're lying. You'd do anything to break up me and Jack. You hate it that I'm with him."

"Huh?" Julian asked. This wasn't going so well.

"You can make up lies all you want. Go ahead, say whatever."

Ellen was madder than ever. Julian couldn't tell if she was *really* mad at him, or upset to hear his news.

"But Ellen, I care about you and I don't want —"

"Just stop!" She *was* mad at him. "I know what you're trying to do. I'm sorry . . . I just don't love you."

Right before Ellen's eyes, Julian fell to pieces.

CHAPTER FOUR

What have I done? Ellen wondered as she woke up the next morning. *I can't believe I snapped and said that.* Her stomach was an empty pit — she knew she had hurt him. She would just have to talk to him and get this straight. And hopefully, he'd pull himself together. Julian always managed to come back and take his place as the too-cool best friend he was meant to be. But the scene kept playing in her brain. Julian ripping the tape out of the VCR and rushing out of her house in a pathetic attempt to hide his tears. It was too intense, and it made Ellen feel — she couldn't describe it — funny. She'd call him tomorrow. She needed to apologize, but it was all just too weird and upsetting. Yes, she'd make it up to him tomorrow. For now, she tried to push it all out of her mind.

Right now, she had another problem.

If she was going to have sex, Ellen needed to prepare. Ellen wasn't ashamed that she planned to spend one day of her life doing what her sister always did — primping like a beauty queen. Ellen wanted everything to be even more perfect and seductive than it sounded on those sappy R&B songs. Yes, Ellen's night would be special. Just like her life, which included two great best friends, a model-hot boyfriend, good grades, and pretty damn cool parents (well, usually). Aside from that tiff with Julian and her butthole sister, Ellen had a life she could get high on. Tonight would just make everything even better — especially since she had every detail of the whole entire thing planned out. It was impossible for anything to go wrong.

See, she'd arrive at Jack's big party and be the epitome of coolness. Ellen was never the type to have a ferret when other people didn't like her — in fact it was quite the opposite, she liked things that way. What on earth would Ellen have to say to a bunch of cheer squeakers who only cared about the newest types of shine shampoo and the latest gossip on who's doing who? Popular people weren't nearly as deep as Julian, which explained why he got so upset last night. And as much as Melisha was a clique-monger, at least she was just as worried about getting into a good college as Ellen was. Somehow Jack seemed different, too — he always seemed so smart and emotional to Ellen — even though he *was* high profile. Ellen basked in the fact that she, last year's spelling bee winner, had snagged every pimple-fighting, stuffed-bra girl's most-wanted man.

She was going to work it tonight. She figured everyone at Jack's party would be polite to her for Jack's sake, but she knew she wouldn't be able to carry on conversations with people for long. That's why Melisha would be there — Melisha already volunteered to rescue Ellen from bizarro party fouls (last weekend, a guy called Burp lost a tooth after trying to open a beer can with his mouth, and everybody had to help him look for it). Plus, Melisha always gave Ellen good Shitville High publicity — Melisha was chatty, funny, and, well, popular.

Ellen already told her parents that she was spending the night at Melisha's, so when the party was over (Melisha said she'd try to lure everyone out early by suggesting they go get Eggs Over My Hammy at Denny's), Ellen would make her move. She had her virginity-losing backpack all ready. It was well-stocked with Altoids, two Bath and Body love-scent candles, matches, a tasteful purple Victoria's Secret teddy, Class Act condoms, K-Y (she didn't want her first time to hurt), and a cute Eve-like outfit for tomorrow morning. (Yes, Jack's dad was out of town.)

Five o'clock on the dot, the phone rang. "Hello — it's for *me*, Evil," Ellen said when she heard someone on the other phone.

"Hey, babe, come on over. I need you to help me put all of this beer in the refrigerator," Jack said.

"See you in five," Ellen said as she glanced in the mirror and grabbed her red backpack.

Intrigued by her sister's out-of-character behavior, Eve dashed into Ellen's room just as she heard the front door slam shut. *Hmmm*, Eve thought as she reached into Ellen's file cabinet. Just as she remembered from a long time ago, Ellen's journal was hiding way in the back of the bottom drawer, behind the file Ellen labeled LETTERS FROM FRIENDS. Eve opened the plain-looking blue spiral notebook and read it, starting at the end.

Tonight's my night. I cannot wait to see what it feels like. I'm so lucky to have such a kick-ass boyfriend to have sex with.

With a crap-eating grin, Eve kept flipping the pages.

If only she knew how much I hate her. How can Mom and Dad not see through her pathetic act? Every nice little thing Eve says has an agenda. If she takes out the trash, it's because she wants money from Dad so she can go buy her Dexatrim. If she goes to church with Mom, it's because she wants to make out with the preacher's son (which she did last summer in the boys' bathroom). How is it again that we're related?

Eve ripped that page out. But the ones about Ellen dying to lose her virginity were Eve's favorite. She liked them so much that she wasted most of her Saturday night reading the diary. She was briefly interrupted by Julian, who didn't act like a geek for once when he came to take his stuff out of Ellen's room. It dawned on Eve that Ellen's boy toy was kind of cute as he poured his heart out to her. She told him to call her, but she couldn't tell if he really would or not.

Then she headed out the door — Eve had to make a quick appearance at Jack's party to keep up her social status. She carefully "dropped" Ellen's diary next to Heather's yoga tapes. *Whoops!*

By ten P.M., Ellen was overflowing with fury. Still no Melisha — the wench was pulling a no-show on the most important night of Ellen's life. Ellen looked hot, but she felt ridiculous. *Mascara's not meant for me*, she thought. And to make it worse, no one was talking to her — not even Jack, who was too busy getting all the freshman girls drunk by persuading them to slurp down multiple Jell-O shots. Just then, a smelly skater dude pulled what he thought was a Funkmaster Flex on the one and two. Five minutes later, the drunk DJ banged out a demolition mix of "Intergalactic" while a football player showcased his talent to gleek to the beat. Then Eve came in the door, cruelly causing a scene while she told Ellen how Julian had stopped by and picked up all of his CDs, posters, and movies. That was it. Melisha wasn't answering her phone, and there was no way she could call Julian. She went to Jack's room to watch *Saturday Night Live*. Her big night ended with a few Capris and Jewel doing a somebody-please-smack-her live performance on TV. Ellen fell asleep.

Around midnight, Jack finally came in to check on her. "Be buck in two seconths," he mumbled, obviously tipsy. Ellen quickly got up off his bed and popped three Altoids while she slipped into her purple teddy in record speed. She crawled under the covers. She was so nervous that she hardly noticed the sounds of giggling girls and drunk boys out on Jack's front lawn. Finally, he came back. He hopped into bed smelling like Meisterbrau and started kissing Ellen all over.

"Wait, Jack, wait," Ellen said as she turned down the covers so he could check out her teddy. Turns out, he didn't even notice. He just reached for Ellen's left boob.

"I wanchoo, baby, I wanchoo bad."

Trying to ignore his drunkenness and move toward her ultimate goal of deflowerment, Ellen kissed him passionately — forcing herself to think this was romantic. But Jack kissed her hard and fast — somehow forgetting how much his sweet, soft smooches turned Ellen on. And when they were about to do it, he got clumsy and rough, holding Ellen's wrists down and smashing her with his body. Just when Ellen was about to ask him to be more human about the whole thing, he rolled over. Ellen shook his shoulder — he was slobbering all over the pillow as he snored.

"What the hell?!" Ellen yelled. She got no answer — just louder snoring. Embarrassed, sober, and mad out of her mind,

22

Ellen started hurling things back into her backpack. She put on her clothes, went home, and tried not to cry.

At two in the morning, Ellen carefully opened the front door. She could see the light on in the kitchen. She peeked in, thinking her sister was sneaking a late-night fat-free freezer pop. Instead she caught a glimpse of her mother sitting at the kitchen table, weeping.

Her mom's disturbing behavior disturbed the already-disturbed Ellen. Not wanting to deal, Ellen tiptoed up the steps to her room — which was devoid of cool CDs and posters (those were Julian's). She laid down and began to bawl. Ellen felt so let down and furious. And — even worse — she felt stupid.

CHAPTER FIVE

Aaahhhggg! are terrorists invading *Shitville? Did the purple iMac explode? Did my sister get hit by a Twinkie truck?* Ellen's thoughts were scrambled as she woke to the unusual million-decibel screams going on in her house. "What the — ?" she said to herself as she rubbed caked mascara particles deeper into her eyes and cheeks. Her parents were waging World War III downstairs. She could hear the flying curse words but couldn't make sense of such chaos on a typically quiet Sunday morning at the Hopkins house. She grabbed her remote control to see if anything good was on MTV. *Nope.* So she started to creep out of bed and wash off all the gooky eye makeup when the phone rang.

Glad for a distraction, Ellen picked up the receiver before one full *dingaling* was complete.

"Hey, baby." Jack's voice was weak.

Ellen wondered if he'd been blowing drunken chunks all night. *Grrr.* She hoped so.

"I want to come pick you up." He sounded awful.

"And why should I —" Ellen stopped talking when she heard the unspeakable F-word come out of her father's mouth.

24

Jack chimed in with, "I want you to come over for breakfast or lunch or something."

"Um, be here in five minutes. My parents are fighting big-time downstairs."

"Man, that sucks. I'll be there in three."

"Give me a second to shower," Ellen replied.

"Nah, you can do that over here." She could hear his smirk through the phone lines.

Ellen let his last comment slide and did a thirty-second shower. She even brushed her teeth under the Massage-O-Matic. She wouldn't have let Jack off the hook like that but she wanted to sneak the hell out of the Bates Motel. It was just too hectic at her house — somebody could get knifed or something. Still unnoticed by her parental powers that be, she threw on some half-clean jeans and a tank top. She grabbed her red backpack just in case Jack's apology was good.

Ellen wrote a note saying she went to Jack's and that she'd be right back. She taped it to the hall telephone and waited at the end of her driveway. Jack was doing pretty well for a hungover guy — he showed up right away.

She hopped in the car, looked at Jack (he was so cute, he immediately made her sweat), and attempted to give him the silent treatment.

"C'mon, Ellen. I don't even know what happened last night. I don't have a clue," Jack said.

Ellen looked at him again (*ohmigod what gorgeousness*). But she stuck to her strategy: silence.

"Ellen, God. You are hot today." Jack was trying the sweet-talk approach. Plus, she did look good. *I have to have her,* Jack thought.

His wooing was working. Ellen couldn't help but smile at him.

He pulled into the McDonald's driveway. "Ain't nothin' like a Super Size after a night like last night. This okay with you?"

"Yeah," she said.

Progress, he thought. "Look, I'm, uh, sorry. I don't know why I acted like such an asshole," Jack said while ordering two Number Twos.

They dined on the back porch of Jack's house. He held her hand, touched her face, and kissed her.

Yep, he's forgiven. Ellen followed Jack into his beer-smelling bedroom. This time, she was so incredibly excited about it. *Finally, finally, finally,* she thought.

The Let's-Get-It-On games began when Jack turned on an R. Kelly CD, and they fell onto Jack's bed. Ellen was impressed — Jack had skills when he was sober. And Jack, well, he knew what he was doing.

That's when it happened. At first, Ellen didn't notice. She got out her do-it gear — condoms and K-Y — as they sweetly swapped spit. As they sat up so Jack could pull her tank top off, it hit her harder than an upside-down shot of tequila. Her muscles tightened, and she felt sick to her stomach.

"Whose leopard jacket is that on the floor?" she asked as she yanked down her shirt.

"God, I don't know. We had a party here last night, remember?"

Ellen's heart jumped. She stood up and looked down. She

saw Trojan wrappers peeking out from under Jack's bed — Ellen had brought Class Acts. She ran over to the jacket and held it up.

"Are you going psycho? Ellen, come back over here."

She reached into the right pocket of the coat. Sure enough, she found a half-empty pack of bubble gum. It all added up. Julian was right, *damn him*! *DAMN HIM*! "You are so lucky I don't have scissors right now."

"Huh?" Jack didn't get it.

"What's your game? What the hell are you doing with Melisha's jacket on your floor?! She never showed up last night . . . or did she, Jack?" Ellen's voice was urgent — and loud.

"Listen, we had a party last night! Duh! Like I know who all was here," Jack said, annoyed.

"I helped you put all the coats in your dad's room. No one even came in here but me! Or do I have it all wrong?"

Silence. Jack was a dick caught in headlights. He tried to create a quick explanation, something he was usually pretty good at, but nothing came to him. Except that he was immediately disappointed to see Ellen's shirt still covering up her hot body.

Ellen knew what his silence meant: Guilty as Hell. She started throwing everything back into her red backpack. Ellen was fighting tears as she got ready to leave — the second time she'd done that in less than twenty-four hours. But out of nowhere, she went from sad to ravenous.

"My best friend Melisha, Jack? My best freaking friend?" she yelled as she looked him straight in the eye. He stared her down.

"You're jumping to conclusions; we should talk. C'mon, Ellen, please sit down," Jack said.

"You know, Julian told me you were riding Melisha's Love Boat. I'm so brain-dead . . . so clueless," Ellen rambled.

"Yeah, Julian *would* tell you that," Jack said as he mumbled several more mean words.

"What did you say?" Ellen was trying to control her hysterics, but it was hard.

"I *said* Julian is the only loser you'll ever do. I'm not putting up with your I-want-to-wait bullshit anymore. You're not worth it," Jack said.

Not worth it? Ellen thought. *But he told me he loved me!*

Ellen's mind went into complete chaos — her boyfriend was being cruel. Ellen would have preferred a sharp knife to her heart rather than hear him say those words. Her stomach was in a knot and her fingertips were tingling. This was unbelievable. And the hurt was getting worse.

Jack followed Ellen through the house, which scared her. He was being more aggressive than she'd ever seen him.

As she turned the doorknob he said, "You weren't good anyway, Ellen." She kept her head down; she couldn't deal anymore. But before she slammed the door, Jack made it worse. He yelled down the street, "Melisha's hot — hot as hell, Ellen. I'll be workin' it with her in about an hour."

It only took Ellen a second to realize she was completely carless, so she would have to hoof it home. Normally, she'd call Melisha, and Melisha would pick her up and make everything all better. But that wasn't exactly about to happen. Calling

Julian was out, and her battling parents probably didn't even know she was gone. Alone for that three-mile walk home, she let the tears rip. She couldn't get the thoughts out of her head. What did she do to make Jack turn on her so fast? This weekend was supposed to be something special. Ellen, her school's candidate for Most Unlikely to Get Laid, was supposed to experience sex. And she was supposed to have this kick-ass boyfriend when she went back to school on Monday morning. She didn't dream she'd be minus a best friend, too.

The hurt was so intense — she felt physically sick. Her head pounded and her eyes stung from the tears. Her heart nervously throbbed. *This whole thing must be a nightmare*, she told herself. Then she felt her nerves go numb — minutes later, they kicked into overdrive again. Thankfully, though, she had made it home. She wanted to lie down, curl up in a ball, and cry herself to sleep. *Maybe I'll wake up and this whole thing will be over*, she thought.

The house was deadly quiet. At least it seemed like no one was home to harass Ellen in her current state of comatose grief. She struggled up the steps to her room, totally exhausted even though it was only one in the afternoon. Ellen thought about calling Melisha; maybe Melisha could confirm that Jack was lying. Maybe Melisha could set this whole thing straight. Maybe, maybe, maybe . . .

Just as the tears started falling again, Ellen heard a bloodfreezing shriek.

"ELLEN, GET DOWN HERE NOW!"

Shit, Ellen thought. By the sound of her dad's psycho voice, you'd think that Ellen had demolished his new handheld DVD player. Ellen was scared — this was beyond bizarro. She couldn't ever remember hearing her dad sound so mad.

"I SAID NOOOOWWWW!"

Ellen turned around and went back down the steps, propelled by the fear of Ed. She walked into the kitchen, where Heather was also waiting. Ellen's father was pacing at a painfully slow pace — Ellen imagined blood-colored smoke seeping out of his ears and nose. Meanwhile, Heather was slumped over the kitchen table, crying.

"Who died?" Ellen used sarcasm, which was clearly a bad choice. She looked at her mother. Heather was holding Ellen's diary. *Shit, shit, shit.*

"Ellen, go get your red backpack," her dad demanded.

Ellen hesitated. "No."

"GODDAMMIT, I said get it, and bring it down here now."

Heather gasped.

Ellen trudged back up the stairs, her heart beating, beating, beating. She grabbed the backpack and thought about stashing its contents. But her dad surprised her — he was right behind her standing in her doorway. She hoped Heather would help her out with this one. But she was still down in the kitchen.

"Give it to me!" He took it and went down to the kitchen table. Ellen walked into the room just as he was unzipping her now-infamous bag. He lifted out the purple teddy and K-Y jelly. He threw the items on the table and said, "YOU'RE GROUNDED!" Then he left the room. Ellen heard her dad speed away from the house in his Del Sol. She was immediately relieved that her dad was gone. She thought her mom would be more reasonable.

But as Heather cried more, any sort of sympathy from her seemed further and further away. Through her tears, Heather looked Ellen straight in the eyes — with a beady, ballistic expression. "Ellen, you were not brought up this way. I didn't raise a small-town slut."

"What did you say to me?" Ellen was outraged that her mom didn't want to talk this out — and that her mom didn't even attempt to understand.

"I know you heard me."

It took Ellen a second to figure out what was going on. She kept thinking about all the times Heather had told her to write in her journal. *She just wanted to read it,* Ellen thought. Now Ellen wished she could take those words and stuff them down her mother's throat.

"I am so *pissed* that you read my diary. *Pissed!* You're the one who told me to write in it. What is this? A fascist family?" Ellen was roaring angry — and she was losing it.

"Don't you even think about turning this around. I don't want to hear it. And if you use that tone with me —" Heather looked like she might combust. "You are a little —"

"Oh, come on, Mom. Come on!" Ellen said, finally backing — and breaking — down. "I swear, this is not what you think." With that, Ellen started bawling. This situation was way more serious than she could handle — especially after being so brutally dumped.

Heather wasn't listening or even paying attention to the hurt her daughter was feeling. She just said, "We have more to worry about than your sex plans. What's all this crap about your sister, Ellen? *You* obviously have low self-esteem, but why do you want to . . . how did you put it? I think you wrote, 'I'd like to pull Eve's fake fingernails out one by one. Slow and painful is the only way to torment Eve.'" Heather cried. "And what about the mean things you wrote about me? What about your dad? Do you hate us that much, too? Do you know how it makes me feel to hear you make fun of my yoga tapes or your dad's car?"

"Mom, Mom, I —"

"You know what? I can't even look at you right now. Go to your room — if you're smart, you won't come out."

Ellen was happy to oblige — she couldn't take the intensity and humiliation for another second. So she ran like hell to her room. The farther away from humanity, the better. She was so cashed that thinking felt like lifting barbells. The beginning of the day with Jack almost seemed like a party compared to this disaster. Well, not quite.

Out of habit, Ellen picked up the phone. Before she had time to realize she had no one to call, she witnessed something even more disturbing than her dad checking out her see-through lingerie:

"I'm so sorry, Heather," the familiar voice on the line said.

"This is awful, just unbelievable," Heather sobbed into the phone.

"Bring that sexy body of yours over, and I'll make it all better. I'll give you ecstasy that'll make you forget this mess. I'll kiss you in places —"

Quietly, quickly, and nauseously, Ellen put down the phone. The voice unmistakably belonged to Mr. Cruz — her English teacher. Her mother was supposed to go over there for a "yoga" class in about two hours.

32

An affair? AN AFFAIR?! Just when Ellen thought nothing could surprise her ever again, she discovered this psychotic bit of information.

Fury. Sadness. Confusion.

Ellen couldn't deal.

CHAPTER SIX

It's about ten feet *long and ten feet wide. And grayish white. You can lock yourself in or out. There are three ways to escape. It has been everything from a battlefield to a hideout to Makeout Central. And I'm stuck here — forever. Sentenced to life — two never-ending weeks — in my room. It's only been three hours. I've got three hundred and thirty-three hours left. That boils down to nineteen thousand, nine hundred and eighty minutes. What went wrong?*

I'm going to kill myself.

Maybe I'll drink bleach. Maybe I'll go into my parents' room with a pair of scissors and cut myself to shreds. I bet Mom and Dad would feel bad about all of this then. And Melisha and Jack would hear and never get over it, either. Julian would be forever haunted about not helping me through this. And Eve, well, Eve would throw a party — even though this is all her fault. Diaries don't just land on top of old-fart yoga tapes. I should cut her up before I do it to myself.

With her last sentence, Ellen ripped the page out of her notebook. She didn't need her ramblings read, so she laid on her bed and tore the paper over and over. After a short period of feeling okay, she started to get upset again. She spent the next hour tearing the innocent piece of paper into four hundred minuscule pieces while tears fell one after another down her cheeks. She ripped out another piece and another, mutilating them, too — tears still coming — while she listened to Bert and Ernie sing her favorite little-kid song, "Rubber Ducky," again and again and again.

Ellen was losing it. She was desperate to call Julian — but couldn't bring herself to do it. She was so alone. And her house was empty — her dad had vanished; Heather had gone to "yoga" lessons; Eve was out doing anything to avoid Ellen — but still, Ellen wouldn't leave her room. She was so psychotically upset that she couldn't even walk. She couldn't turn on the TV. She couldn't even *think* about watching E! or reading her brand-new *Spin*.

Her mind was working in sound bites. One second she thought about Jack — the next she'd think about Melisha — the next she'd see her dad inspecting her K-Y do-it lube — the next she'd hear her mother call her a slut — then she'd have a mental picture of Heather humping Mr. Cruz. Everything was churning, making her mind feel like a crazy factory. Then the nausea took over.

She couldn't see how any of this would ever get better. EVER. She didn't know if her life would be fun or easy ever again. No boyfriend. No best friends. No parents. No life.

Drunk from crying, she finally fell asleep on top of her *Bell Jar* bits of paper.

*   *   *

"Ellen, get up." The voice was ice-cold. But still, Ellen sat up straight, obeying orders like a plebe in boot camp.

"God, you're impossible," Heather said as she surveyed the mess in Ellen's room. "You'd do *anything* to make me miserable, wouldn't you?"

Unconsciously, Ellen gave her the saddened, empty look of a whipped puppy. But Heather wasn't even facing Ellen — she couldn't stand the sight of her older daughter.

Looking into the mirror, Heather said, "You won't be going to school tomorrow. Eve will pick up your assignments."

Ellen just stared at the torn pieces of paper.

"I already called my gynecologist at home, and you're going in tomorrow."

Ellen gasped. "No, I don't nee —"

"ELLEN!" Heather surprised herself with her harsh tone. "You're going. I'm not having a pregnant teen in my house! Dr. Clipper said she'd examine you and give you the morning-after pill — it's good up to seventy-two hours after sex."

Ellen started to cry again. She wanted to scream that she knew all about Heather's affair. But she just didn't have an ounce of energy left so she didn't dare open her mouth.

Heather eyed the red backpack. Ellen thought Heather might take it, but she didn't. After what felt like three hours, Heather left the room. Ellen got up off the bed and hit play. "Rubber Ducky" filled the room once again.

"Really?" Melisha said to Jack. They had just finished the body boogie on Jack's bed.

Jack nodded yes, but he wasn't looking at Melisha.

"You told her she wasn't nearly as hot-damn as I am?"

Melisha said as she rubbed Jack's chest and twirled her curly hair. She was thinking about how she really needed to put some hair masque on her mane before school tomorrow.

"I told her, and I'm all yours, baby," Jack said while looking at the television.

"Now we can play Ping-Pong every single day, sweetie." Melisha's smile was genuine when she said it.

Jack wasn't really listening to her. He was preoccupied with the fact that his team, Notre Dame, was kicking Michigan's butt.

Melisha was patient with him for a few minutes. Then she whipped out some star-style seduction to make sure Jack gave *her* another round of attention.

CHAPTER SEVEN

It was Tuesday morning: also known as Ellen's Armageddon. If she could choose, Ellen would go back to the crotchety old gynecologist a thousand times instead of going back to Shitville High. As she thought about it, she cried some more on her snot-covered pillowcase. But she knew there would be no escape — playing sick would do her no good while her parents had a Get-Ellen agenda. So Ellen kept visions of the movie *Carrie* (the original) in her head to make herself feel better. But as she jumped out of the shower, she just felt like a *Welcome to the Dollhouse* Wiener Dog.

Yes, life is hell.

And it got worse because Ellen had to ride to school with her sister. There was nobody left to pick up Ellen — it was Eve or the school bus. Ellen almost chose the beyond-embarrassing bus but Heather forced Ellen to leave with Eve. Once in the car, Ellen popped in a Cure tape and turned it up. She didn't want to sit next to the bitch, let alone speak to her. So the two sisters remained silent. Meanwhile, Ellen tried to will a semi to slam into the driver's side. It didn't. They got to Shitville High in one piece, and Eve happily bounced into school in plenty of time to catch the morning's gossip. Ellen sat in the car and smoked a Capri. She was late to first period on purpose.

"Miss Hopkins," the teacher said as Ellen slipped into her seat. Her heart tripled its tempo. "It's nice to see you. I hope you can remember when class starts from now on." Ellen could feel everyone's eyes light-sabering straight through her. To make things worse, Ellen turned rashy red. But about fifteen minutes into class, enough time for everyone to have forgotten all about her, people were still eyeing Ellen. They were whispering even. She kept her head down and visualized *Carrie*. Some sick joke was hanging in the classroom air — and Ellen didn't get it. She didn't like feeling like a dork inbred. But she did, and the whole unspoken situation was about to make her cry.

Then a phantom note landed on Ellen's desk. She had no clue who wrote it — she wasn't down with anyone in that class. It was folded origami-style, so it took Ellen a second to open it up.

It read:

Ellen,
Girl, you've got problems. Your ditzy sister's butt-breath friend Sara Whatever-her-name-is spread a raunchy rumor about you yesterday. She said you got wasted and danced bare-ass naked in front of that dick-wrinkle Jack at his party this weekend. According to her, you were begging to get laid, and he refused to do you. It doesn't end there, though. I heard he bounced your best friend instead. (Guess she's not your girl anymore, huh?) Anyway, I think that sucks, and I wanted you to know what was going down about you. Whatever the truth really is, I don't think it's fair that no one asked you for your side of the story. And well,

you weren't here yesterday, so the whole school was cracking up about it. That clique is so whack. I'm sorry they're talking shit about you, that's all. If you need anything, give me a shout-out.

Peace,
Meg

Ellen had to reread the note for the words to seep through her brain. At first, she thought it must be a mistake. No one would think she really danced naked . . . and was going to have sex . . . and got wasted? Ellen wasn't exactly a party-perfect sort of girl. That's not to say she, Melisha, and Julian hadn't had a few private bashes. But usually Ellen kept such a low profile that she was surprised anyone cared at all. And they probably wouldn't have if Jack wasn't in the whole warped picture.

She pored over the letter a fourth time. Ellen had thought her emotional pain threshold had been crossed already. But she had been so wrong. She still managed to feel a black hole of hurt when she read that note. She didn't even know the girl who wrote it, she just knew the girl was a Coma — one of those weird kids who wore a lot of black makeup and red lipstick. But that didn't matter — Ellen knew the note was right on target — she could hear people whispering and laughing. She raised her hand and asked for a hall pass with such urgency that her teacher was afraid to tell her no.

Ellen dashed to the bathroom and began to lose her breath. She was fighting the grapefruit-sized lump that had crept its way up her esophagus. She reread Meg's letter two more times. Then she flushed it down the toilet and forced herself to go back to class.

✻   ✻   ✻

Julian. Julian. Julian. His name was a scratched CD that kept repeating itself in her mind. He was the only person who might still be persuaded to give a crap. She had to talk to him and beg him to pull her sorry ass through this. She needed him to cheer her up with his dumb jokes, ego-boosting puppy love, and nightly phone calls. She would make it up to him somehow. She'd never needed a best friend more than she needed one now. If she just told him what hell her life was, he'd understand the stupidity of their fight. He'd see that they could make up and move on.

She kept scoping him out with no luck. Obviously, he was allergic to *her* today. She finally pinned him down during lunch. He tried to walk the other way, but she cornered him.

Face-to-face, Ellen didn't know what to say. She just stood there burning holes into his nervous eyes. "Julian, give me a chance. . . ."

"What the hell do you want?"

Ellen was startled by his reaction. He had never sounded so sick of her before.

"I really need to talk, Julian. My whole life is on heroin."

"It's always about you, Ellen. *Always*. You crash, and I'm supposed to pick up the pieces."

"No, this is about *you*. I need you!"

"You only need me so *you'll* feel better. Well, guess what? You lose." Julian couldn't look at Ellen — saying these things hurt him more than she knew. But he had made a pact with himself earlier to move on — to try to get over Ellen Hopkins once and for all. "No more Ellen pity parties for me. I'm sick of it. You don't even call me until your other friends dump you first."

"That's so not true," Ellen replied. She was stunned.

"Isn't it, though? Didn't my psychic Melisha-and-Jack prediction come true?" he said as he tugged at his usual uniform, a wrinkled blue Gap button-down with a white T-shirt underneath. "Now you want to talk to me *after* you made a fool of yourself at his party? I don't think so, Ellen. If everything had gone your way, you wouldn't be standing here pleading with me right now."

"Come on, tell me you don't believe that." *Pleading with him?* Ellen thought. She could hardly admit it to herself but that was exactly what she was doing. She didn't know what else to do. Usually, it was so easy to get Julian to come around. Today, though, for the first time in their history, the two of them just weren't jibing.

"Why would I think anything else, Ellen? You haven't turned out to be anything I thought you were."

Ellen was shocked. *Is this my best friend Julian?* "What? You know me better than anyone. I just haven't been myself lately. C'mon, Julian, I don't know what to do!" Ellen was saying just about anything to change his mind, and she was shamelessly begging him to give her another chance. Julian was her only hope; without him, she was completely isolated from the rest of the world.

"Look, Ellen. Let's just leave it alone. I don't really *need* you anymore." Julian lifted his head and looked down the hall. His nonchalant act worked — Ellen thought he looked more confident than she had ever seen him.

Ellen swallowed his words about as easily as a dose of Alka-Seltzer. She choked nervously.

"I've got other friends, you know," Julian said, without his usual sneeze-induced twitching. Ellen didn't even see a sign of his inhaler — he had put it somewhere other than his jeans pockets. "I might even be seeing someone. I'm actually having fun since we stopped talking. Look, I don't think you and I should be cool with each other for a while."

"I'm alone, though," Ellen said quietly, nearly in tears.

Julian shook his head and walked off. The scene was more than he could take.

The bell rang, and Ellen was late again. This time for English — the one class she looked forward to as much as her next face-to-face with her dad. And there he was, Mr. Cruz, *The Freak Show Who Has Sex with My Mother*. Her sadness over Julian temporarily faded. Instead, she felt enraged — a cheeseball English teacher was trying to rip her family apart. And she still had to attend his class. She walked into the room, gave him a dirty look, and sat down.

"Ellen, please tell me what last night's reading was about. I gave the assignment to your sister if I remember correctly."

Of course, Eve hadn't given Ellen a thing.

Ellen didn't say a word; she let her eyes do the talking for her.

"Oh, so school isn't important to you anymore, I see." Mr. Cruz was being unusually cruel. "I'd like you to write a two-page summary of the literary technique that Langston Hughes uses in the piece. I'd like it on my desk by eight A.M."

The rest of the class gasped. They couldn't believe Mr. Cruz would be so evil.

"Did you hear me, Ellen?"

She said yes with as much hostility as she could muster. But she complied — drawing *more* attention to herself was the last thing she needed today. She could hear the pom-pom captain calling her a wanna-be guest on *Ricki Lake* from the other side of the room.

Nice. Maybe I've just got some really sucky karma, Ellen thought at the same time she wished cellulite on the bitch cheerleader.

Seeing how well the entire school day was going, Ellen decided to skip the rest of her classes. What were her parents going to do, ground her? *Wish I cared*, Ellen thought. She headed to the girls' rest room way out by the school's crappy track field. She rubbed her temples, wiped her eyes, and sat on the toilet seat thinking about a lot of nothing. Just before last period, that Meg girl, the one who wrote the note, showed up. Ellen came out of the stall when she smelled the cigarette smoke.

"Hey," Meg said, smoke escaping through her mouth and nose. She was checking out her infected nose ring in the mirror while pushing her banana-yellow bangs out of her face.

"Oh, yeah, hi," Ellen replied. "Can I smoke one of those?"

The girls hung out for about five minutes saying less than three words.

When Meg left, Ellen followed her. Ellen decided that going to last period was better than sitting on a crusty, fifty-year-old toilet seat feeling sorry for herself.

"One day, I'm gonna quit," Meg said as she stuffed her mouth full of Gobstoppers. She handed Ellen a few of them. The jawbreakers were green and blue.

CHAPTER EIGHT

Ellen walked into the cafeteria on Wednesday of the worst week of her life. She had her usual lunch fare — a turkey sandwich with Cheez Balls, an apple, and a pack of Ho-Hos. She braved the cafeteria for the first time since the trauma began, but only because it was pouring outside. Her new spot out by the tennis courts was soaked.

She prayed that Meg would be in there eating, since she would be forced indoors today, too. Ellen didn't know Meg — or her freaky Coma friends — all that well. She hoped they'd be kind enough to save her from the most humiliating possibility in all of high school: sitting solo during lunch. Ellen walked into the huge silver-and-blue glass-enclosed room with her head high. She made like she knew what she was doing. But there was no Meg in sight. Ellen had no clue what to do next. She got shaky as she walked between the narrow tables looking for somebody, *anybody* she might know.

She spotted Melisha and Jack. For the moment, the world stopped. The panic of going it alone in the cafeteria didn't seem like as big of a deal in comparison. There they were, all happy and obnoxious. There Ellen was, all ruined and utterly miserable. She hated them with the deepest, blackest hate. Who were they to turn her life upside down, then flaunt it in her face? Who were they to act happy in her presence? Hate turned to hurt. The biggest imaginary knife in the world was hacking her in the heart over and over and over again. She stood perfectly still, paralyzed by her emotions.

But, unfortunately, the earth started rotating again, and that horrible lunchroom came back into focus. Abruptly, Ellen realized that on top of everything else, she was still alone in the lunchroom, all eyes on her. She tried to be slick, like she didn't care even though she did, and tried to turn in the opposite direction of her two exes. To make things as humanly embarrassing as possible, some bitch tripped her. It was Eve and her friends. They started whispering and laughing. Ellen thought she heard them talking about her diary. *Does the whole school have to know about that, too?*

Of course, the whole jock clan — Melisha and Jack included — turned around, pointing at "Ellen the naked dancing queen!" At that moment, Ellen dropped her snack cakes. Another round of laughter ensued once the evil, teen-packed room could see that her snacks were called Ho-Hos. Their comments were not of the kind variety. She turned bloodred and ran for the cafeteria door as everyone cackled.

When she got to the exit, a hand grabbed her shoulder. "Young lady, no food will be taken out of the cafeteria." She looked up and Mr. Cruz's cootie-hand was on her arm. She shook it off violently.

"Don't even think about touching me," Ellen said. "What a perfect day for you to be on lunch duty."

"Yes, isn't it?" Mr. Cruz replied with a sneaky smirk.

Ellen kept right on walking — she didn't dream that this loser would bother her. But he did — he grabbed her shoulder a second time.

"I don't think that's the proper way to treat a teacher, Ellen. I want you to sit right here," he said as he walked back into the cafeteria and pushed her shoulder down at the school employee table.

Ellen saw everyone looking at her but sat down silently. As Mr. Cruz left, she said, "Oh, thanks so much . . . Guy." She was so mortified and pissed — plus, she was trying to recover from those imaginary knife wounds. It's no wonder that she couldn't even touch her turkey sandwich, no matter how hungry she might have been. The thought of eating made her ill, so she threw it in the trash once lunchtime was over.

Ellen dipped further into an angry depression as the days passed. She decided that a lifetime of breakouts would have been better than becoming Shitville High's hot gossip topic of the week. Ellen was the object of humiliation. To top it all off, she hadn't spoken more than ten words to anybody since Sunday morning. The only time she said a word was when Meg offered her a cigarette in the faraway bathroom or when a teacher called on her to answer some dumb-ass question. Ellen wasn't out to become a social recluse. But if she didn't speak, no one could yell at, laugh at, dis, or hurt her.

Being strong — or something like that — was beyond lonely. Ellen missed her old life, the one where she was in demand, not in the doghouse. The worse part was, not one of her so-called friends had even tried to contact her. Most surprisingly, Julian hadn't caved in — Ellen thought he would've called for sure. In fact, Ellen didn't even *see* Julian around school. It was like he had vanished from Indiana. She told herself she didn't care — he was just a goob, anyway. And hinting he had a girlfriend? *Whatever*. Melisha didn't call, either. Ellen couldn't believe Melisha owned the other half of her fourth-grade treasure, her Best Friends Forever necklace. *What a waste*, Ellen kept thinking. And as much as it made her mad, Ellen missed Jack, too. Sure, he turned out to be butt-slime, but in his pre-prick days, he was really cool. It didn't help Ellen's sad state of mind to see Melisha and Jack put on a daily PDA show in the high school hallway, either.

Clearly, it was Ellen who was coming up short in the pal department. She had never even noticed that her friends only numbered three. She just knew that she used to be sooo happy. Now, though, even her mom wasn't speaking to her. Being a friendless free agent wasn't fun.

Ellen was sure she'd be alone for the rest of her life.

Friends was over. All of those shiny, happy, skinny people reminded Ellen that she was starving. Her family was downstairs pigging out on Papa Joe's Slice of Heaven, laughing and having fun. Ellen figured they were just thrilled because she was tucked away in her room — not complicating their lives. So Ellen sat at the top of the stairs listening and waiting for everyone to finish so she could tiptoe into the kitchen and steal the leftovers without causing any family fireworks.

She lost her appetite, though, as she listened to their sickening conversation.

"I just *can't* believe it. Un-*be*-liev-*a*-ble, that's what it is," Eve chirped. "I'm just so glad that Drewcilla is in rehab. There's no way that she'll be allowed to compete in Miss Corncob."

"That's too bad for her — but good for you," Dad said.

"What?! You mean you think she could have beat *me*?!!!"

"Calm down, Eve," Heather chimed in. "You're gorgeous; you know your dad and I think you'll win hands down."

With that, Ellen almost gagged and went back to her room. *Your dad and I? What a joke. Heather's a cheater from hell. And Eve's just evil — maybe I'll Nair her head while she's asleep.* Ellen tiptoed back up the stairs and opted for her hidden can of Cheez Balls.

It was three A.M. and sleeping would have been easier if hungry hyenas were trampling through Ellen's bedroom. She'd already watched her family's *Grease* video three times in a row. That used to cheer her up . . . but apparently, even in large doses, the sugar-sweet story and tunes could not adjust Ellen's mood. Nor could she escape from her private hell.

Ellen had no interest in eating or smoking. Everything in life that used to be enjoyable had lost its luster — even Phish Food. Numbness overtook every nerve in her body.

She had to get up for school in less than four hours, so she finally lay down and turned out her lights. Forcing sleep might be the only escape from her miserable world. She turned on her favorite Barenaked Ladies CD again and put the repeat button on the song "Old Apartment," because it made her cry every time she heard it. She was hoping she'd finally slip into sleep from sheer tear exhaustion.

CHAPTER NINE

Ellen didn't sleep a wink. She felt like one of those cartoon zombies, the ones whose eyes are buzzing in never-ending circles, as she lolled back into her house after school. The whole day was blurry. She snuck some zzzs in most of her classes — and of course, Mr. Cruz took it upon himself to kick her desk leg, jolting it really hard while she was getting some serious, drool-worthy shut-eye. Mr. Cruz was waging some kind of sick, twisted war with Ellen — and she hated him so much that she'd die if he won it.

Meg noticed Ellen's dozing and slipped her a pair of Mini Thins in the bathroom. But instead of making Ellen electric with energy, the bad little pills caused her to pee every five minutes. Ellen almost went to the nurse to feign sickness. She figured she might as well use her wetting episodes as an excuse to go home early. Then she remembered that the most miserable place in the world was her house.

But now another worthless day at school was over, and Ellen was forced to head home. She had big plans for the weekend. Starting tonight, she was going to hit the repeat button on her Hole CD and spend the next 48-plus hours in bed with a box of

Puffs Plus. Yep, that was the order of the evening. She figured she might switch CDs once a day or so. She also wanted to see how bad she could possibly stink, so she declared it a bath-free weekend (it had already been two days).

As she walked up to the steps, she heard a voice — someone was actually speaking to her.

"Ellen, clean yourself up," her mother called from the kitchen. "Tonight's the Miss Corncob pageant."

Since no one had spoken to her for days, Ellen was hoping she was out of the loop on that one. She'd honestly forgotten that it was *this* fun-filled weekend.

"I thought I was grounded."

"Oh, you *are*. That's why you're going to this — and sitting with me."

Like I had anyone else to sit with, Ellen thought.

Thankfully, Eve was already gone. She had to be at the Miss Stupidwench Rehearsal earlier that day.

"Fix yourself up. We have to get going in an hour!"

Hey, Mom, how are those yoga lessons coming? Ellen didn't dare say it out loud. But she sure as hell didn't have to wonder why Heather had been gone a lot lately. Ellen couldn't believe that she used to look up to her mom — she used to be *close* to her. That fact alone was a testimonial to how much Ellen's life had changed since last weekend.

"Did you hear me?" Heather yelled.

"Yes." Ellen trudged up the stairs and lay down on her bed. She sure as hell wasn't going to waste her Tone body wash on her sister's Little Miss Lightbulb Extravaganza.

At five till time-to-go, Ellen willed herself off of her bed and threw on a half-dirty pair of khakis (*I've only worn 'em four or five times. . . .*) with a tank top. She briefly looked in the mirror and readjusted her bubbly ponytail. She overlooked two scabby zits that were still red from yesterday's pathetic pick session.

Ellen was delusional. Maybe it was her lack of sleep, but her thought patterns weren't running on a full canister of Cheez Balls. She actually thought she looked pretty decent, all things considered. She flipped off her CD player, headed down the steps, and got into her mother's car.

Heather got into the car. Ellen noticed how nervous her mother looked. It was weird because she used to be the rock of stability. Heather just glanced at Ellen, shaking her head at her messy "other" daughter.

All too soon, they arrived at the school auditorium, where the *she*bang was just starting to take place. Heather ran backstage to help Eve create cleavage by taping her boobs together and stuffing the vacant sides. They were early, so Ellen moseyed back to her favorite bathroom outside near the track.

"Damn," Ellen said to herself when she found out the girls' room was locked. Then another voice surprised her — she had thought she was alone.

"Suck a pork sausage." Apparently, someone else had wanted inside that bathroom, too.

Ellen looked behind her and Meg was standing there. She had a small bottle of rubbing alcohol in one hand and an unopened pack of cigarettes in the other. She had two packs of Gobstoppers — one under each arm.

"Hey," Ellen said unenthusiastically, even though she was kind of glad to run into someone who didn't wish zits on her.

"C'mon, nobody's here. Let's just go behind the building."

"'Kay."

Meg lit two cigarettes at once. And even though they were Camel Lights, Ellen still took one. Meg mumbled her usual spiel about quitting. Then Meg told Ellen she hated this kind of sexist display of antifeminism, but her second cousin was a contestant so her mom made her come. Ellen, still feeling zombie-ish, stayed quiet.

"What's with you? I know things at school blow lately, but it seems like you're living in another dimension," Meg asked while she put some alcohol on the infected spot where her nose ring hung.

"I'm just, whatever."

"Well, stop acting like you think you're a smelly sack of cow shit. If you think that, everyone else will, too. At least that's my philosophy."

"Uh-huh." *Whatever*, Ellen thought.

"You don't get it, girl. I don't think that." They sucked on their Camels and walked into the auditorium in silence.

The place was packed to the rotting air-conditioner vents. It looked like a Miss America contest instead of a small-town pageant for popular pretty girls. The entire town was in full effect for the evening. And of course, the homecoming-queen crowd reigned over the back four rows. Ellen got queasy knowing she'd have to walk past everyone to sit with her parents, who were parked front row center. So she put her head down and started her trek, passing Melisha and Jack first. Her peripheral vision told her they were looking her way and sharing a secret. She also noticed that they had their hands all over each other.

As she walked by she heard Melisha's voice. "Just call her smellin' Ellen. That girl should be borrowin' my Ivory."

All of a sudden, it dawned on Ellen that she probably looked like a greaseball. *Guess it would matter if somebody actually gave a cat's ass,* Ellen thought. *Not a soul here can stand me anyway. Not my would-have-been friends. Not the rest of Shitville High. Not my parents. Well, at least they're biologically required to sit by me.* She pitied herself all the way up the row, just to find out that her seat next to Heather was taken. Mr. Cruz was hamming it up with her parents! Right in front of her father!

Heather nervously shooed Mr. Cruz — she called him by his sicko first name, Guy — and he got up to leave, giving Ellen a mean look as he brushed past her. Ellen sat down and scratched her pimples. Her nerves were on acid. She didn't know what to do about anything but she knew she *had* to do something about Mr. Cruz. Oh, and Heather, too. She couldn't just sit by brooding while they went behind everyone's back. No matter what Ellen had — or hadn't — done, she knew what her mom was doing was a lot worse.

And with that, the curtain came up. Ten girls in cat costumes — black shiny leotards with long red tails — hit the stage, singing and dancing à la troupe. They were doing some sort of psychotic rendition of a Jellicle cats song from the musical *Cats*.

The pain and suffering continued during the talent show, where one girl had the nerve to do an X-rated acrobat routine. She did a back walkover, landed in the splits, then proceeded to put both of her legs behind her head.

Ugh.

Eve sounded okay when she sang "Memory."

What a suck-up. That amoeba chose another song from Cats *just to ass-kiss those judges.*

The brain parade would be showing off their evening gowns next. The contortionist wore a see-through number that unflatteringly displayed her nipples. Eve was in a straight sequined mermaid dress that made the crowd gasp when she walked onto the stage. On the outside, she really was stunning. Too bad the inside was all rotten.

Ellen tried to tune out the girls when the emcee started asking the contestants questions. It didn't work.

"Julie, what's your stance on AIDS awareness in the new millennium?"

"Well, Ms. Judge, I'd like to say that it's a sad, sad, sad thing that brings me to tears just *thinking* about it. All of those poor gay people! Oh! I would make the world chicken soup!" Everyone applauded, except Ellen.

Is that girl on drugs?

"Eve, what would you do to encourage world peace?"

"I would start a campaign for kindness. I would travel the country, getting all the nation's important people to sign a peace petition. Then I'd take it to Washington, D.C., myself."

I feel a bowel movement coming on.

But at least Ellen was getting off on mind-dissing everyone; it was an underrated guilty pleasure. Sure, it was a little mean. That's why Ellen kept her thoughts to herself.

After three excruciating hours, the curtain finally went down.

"The third runner-up is Becky Lebodee!" the emcee announced as the bouncy sophomore ran up to her, crying and hugging.

55

They announced the second and first runner-ups — Eve got neither award. Ellen was keeping her fingers crossed; she'd want to die if the bitch won. At least the weirdo acrobat cow wasn't winning anything.

Then the winner was announced: "Eve Hopkins!"

Never mind, I was lying — I don't want to die. But she's still a lugie-licker.

Ellen was surprised that her sister actually accomplished something besides giving out her phone number to innocent boy victims. Heather and Ed jumped out of their seats, minus any inkling of yoga-esque grace. They were drooling with excitement. The whole school seemed happy with the choice of winner, too.

Yes, the gods are cruel.

Eve did the whole bit — she cried, put on a sorry excuse for a small-town crown, and donned her golden-colored Miss Corncob pageant ribbon. She gave fake hugs to the girls on stage who smiled but couldn't hide their deep, jealous hatred. Then she walked toward the crowd to act giddy with all of her friends.

A boy ran up first to give Eve a dozen yellow roses. Ellen hoped to thief one because they were her favorite flowers. But. What. Happened. *Deep breath.* Next. Um. Shocked. Ellen. Beyond. *C'mon, I can't faint.* Um. Belief.

The boy Eve was kissing, the one who gave her the yellow roses . . . well, his name was Julian.

And he used to call Ellen "Elle."

CHAPTER TEN

The pageant had been a big fat blur of consciousness. It was so unreal that the next morning Ellen was remembering everything in worn-out, faded colors. It was dreamlike — only she was too exhausted to make it memorable. She bolted up from her daybed, looked around, and realized her recollections, no matter how sketchy, were totally real.

Eve was in fact the new Miss Corncob — a title she was bound to wear with ego-boosting arrogance. That's not all, though — the pretty, pukey parasite was also putting the moves on Julian. It wasn't enough that the gorgeous bimbo had already trashed Ellen's rep both at home *and* school. She also took it upon herself to steal Ellen's most devoted friend and turn him against her.

Ellen's thoughts were interrupted when the phone rang. She picked it up with a sixth sense that it would be Julian.

"Hello," Ellen said. *Yep, I was right.*

"I'm calling for Eve," the boy said nervously. He had a feeling Ellen would pick up, but it was hard to tell because she and her sister sounded so much alike.

"Julian, listen —" Ellen said as fast as she could.

"Just tell me if Eve's there."

"I really want us to be friends again. Don't you miss me?" Ellen was pleading at this point.

"The question is, do you really miss *me*? Or are you just pathetically lonely?" he asked her. "Look, I'm having a good time right now. Do you have something against me having fun?"

Ellen felt a pain in her brain. She wanted Julian to have fun more than anything — but with *Eve*? Eve didn't know the first thing about complex guys like Julian. "No, of course not. I just want to know if you *are* happy, Julian."

After an uncomfortable pause he replied, "Of course. I've got more friends than ever before."

"But I know you. You're not like those people."

Cruelly, Eve picked up the phone, successfully interrupting — and ending — the conversation. When she got off the phone, she made a world-class deal out of the school dance later that night. Obviously, Julian would be Eve's date on her beauty-contest-winning debut. Ellen couldn't help but hope that Julian wasn't as excited as Eve sounded. Either way, she knew her former friend would be stressed, and she'd bet one hundred bucks that his allergies were acting up.

He's like a field mouse being hunted down by a Persian, Ellen thought.

Heather had been humming all morning. Ellen, on the other hand, was flat-lining over the whole Julian/Eve thing. Who would've thought that Eve would even speak to Julian, let alone date him? Well, Julian was cute — but Ellen didn't think anyone ever noticed him. Sure, he had porcelain skin that was striking against his dark hair and blue-blue eyes. But he never said a peep, not around anyone but Ellen, Melisha, and a few other girls at school. Julian was so out of the clique-y crowd that those people didn't even consider him a geek — they didn't consider him anything at all. So when Eve started hanging with Julian, he was automatically accepted, like a new boy at school. At least that was Ellen's hypothesis. Regardless, it was all sickening.

Elsewhere in the Hopkins house, the afterglow of Eve's lucky night had everyone high on life. It freaked Ellen out — after one long, horrific week she'd gotten used to being the family pariah. She had come to accept that everyone was pissed at her — and *enjoyed* being pissed at her. Freakiest of all, even her mom was being nice. It was all too weird so Ellen stayed out of the way and quiet. As she sat in her room waiting for everyone to go do something, she realized that the good mood was at least a little contagious — she turned off her Hole CD and put on Madonna.

Heather burst in just as Ellen was getting an itch to take a shower.

"You're ungrounded," Heather said. She didn't roll her eyes or even seem disgusted with Ellen.

"Oh, um, thanks." Actually, it was *good* to be grounded tonight — it was an easy out of the school dance.

"And guess what?" Heather asked.

"Oh boy."

"That means you can go to the dance!"

"No, Heather, forget it. Besides, I didn't put together a costume." Ellen thought she was weaseling out of it. After all, the theme was *That '70s Class* and most girls — including Eve — had been working on their disco gear for weeks.

"Oh, I already dug out some clothes for you, dear."

Dear? What the hell is she calling me dear for? She might have forgiven me, but I haven't even thought about forgiving her. "That's okay, really —"

"Listen, you are going," Heather said. "You have to show support for your sister tonight. Besides, I think it's a much-needed switch for you to go and be civil to Eve rather than sit here all night plotting out ways to kill her." Heather left the room before Ellen could comment.

Ellen turned off Madonna and put on Lords of Acid. She was beginning to realize that this was a sick, twisted part of her parents' punishment. When Heather came back to Ellen's room, she threw a crocheted, multicolored micromini onto the daybed along with a toasted-brown suede shirt that had fringe hanging from the elbows down to the wrist. Last, Heather brought in a pair of white suede, knee-high go-go boots. Ellen was horrified.

"Your dad will take you at nine."

"Dad is taking me? God, can't I take the car?"

"No. Eve needs it to pick up Julian."

"Oh, puh-lease."

"Ellen, if you don't go to this dance with a good attitude, I will ground you for the whole rest of this school year," Heather said as she shut the bedroom door. "Let me see how it looks when you're dressed!" she called from down the hall.

Ellen's heart dropped to her toenails. This. Was. Going. To. Suck.

Surprisingly, the ride with Dad was as painless as it could be. He didn't try to make conversation or eye contact. Ellen bit her tongue — she was dying to tell him about Heather's two-timing tryst. But she decided not to go there, for her dad's sake. Luckily, he just turned up the volume on his new Phish CD. *Thank God*, Ellen thought. Because getting ready with Heather and Eve had been torture enough. They giggled and carried on while crimping Eve's long blondish-brown, highlighted hair. Ellen had nothing else to do but get ready — so she kept herself busy all day with stuff like blue glitter eye shadow and red nail polish. When she was ready to go, Ellen had to admit that she looked damn good (for the first time in a week).

As Ellen approached the gymnasium, she could hear the song "Dancing Queen" blasting over the sound system. She almost fell over when she walked in the door. The dank Shitville High gym had morphed into a full-fledged disco. It was very dark — which hid the stained concrete walls quite well. Besides the good music and serious strobe lights, there was a huge disco ball that must've been bigger than a beanbag chair hanging from the middle of the ceiling. Ellen smiled because it was so cool, then walked over to a snack table, taking each step to the beat of the music. She felt actually, kind of, well, normal for once. . . .

That was until she saw *them*. Right next to the bowl of Sun Chips, Melisha and Jack were dirty dancing while kissing so deeply it looked like they might suffocate. All of a sudden, food didn't sound so good. The total hurt of the past week gurgled inside of her, making her pain feel bigger than the whole gymnasium. While standing there thinking about it, Ellen didn't realize she was staring at the groping couple. Melisha didn't notice, but Jack did. While his lips were on Melisha's, he looked Ellen dead in the eye, moaned, and winked straight at her. Ellen's blood went hot as she ran to the opposite side of the gym.

It's cool, it's cool. I can handle this. I can I can I can I can. Ellen tried to give herself a pep talk as she wiped the tears from her eyes before they had a chance to drip down her cheeks. She cussed out loud when she looked at her fingers — they had blue glitter on them.

"Hey, girl!"

Ellen whipped around to see Meg.

"What are you doing here?" Ellen said, trying to act like she had a cold instead of a crying fit.

Meg didn't buy it. "Oh, c'mon, toots," she said as she grabbed Ellen's hand and squeezed it. "By the way, what the hell are *you* doing here?"

"I wish I knew."

"Me, too. The Barfing Spaghetti concert was canceled tonight, so I came. At least these things always give me a good laugh."

"Oh, yeah," Ellen said cluelessly as she noticed the holes in Meg's fishnets. Meg was so whacked. She had blue stripes in her bright yellow hair, and you could see the black roots popping out of her scalp. Her lipstick was so dark that her lips looked bruised.

"Go put your stuff at my friends' table if you want. I'll be back in a minute," Meg said.

Ellen would have passed but she didn't have anywhere else to sit. Hanging out with a pack of Comas who worship Barfing

Spaghetti wasn't exactly Ellen's idea of a killer time. Regardless, Ellen slung her white suede purse onto her shoulder and headed toward the table. It wasn't easy to miss — a guy named Pearl had his mohawk dyed green and another girl, Harrieta-something, was dressed like a Goth Christina Ricci.

"Hi," Ellen said. They smiled back at her but then resumed their own conversation.

While Ellen pulled out her chair, she saw Eve coming her way, dragging Julian by his hand. They stopped about three feet away from Ellen's table and started dancing. Eve exaggerated her ha-ha-has and grabbed Julian's butt. Ellen noticed how uncomfortable he looked, but she could tell he was trying to be all Romeo. About five seconds later, Eve planted a passionate kiss on him, and all of her friends stood around and cheered.

Just when Ellen was thinking of going out to her trackside bathroom, her table mates asked her to dance.

"Uh, I —" Ellen stuttered.

"C'mon, girlfriend," Pearl said as he pulled her left wrist.

"Sure," she said.

They started headbanging. It didn't matter what song was on. Ellen just closed her eyes and let her body sway to the BeeGees.

Ellen felt her spirit change from angered and hurt to almost self-confident. She liked landing a new group of friends, even if they were a little weird. And she imagined that she was the most successful, smartest, gorgeous girl at Shitville. Then somebody bumped into her. Ellen's fantasies were ruined.

It was Sara, Eve's best friend, dancing right behind her and stepping on Ellen's suede boots. "Ew, yuck," Ellen said as she rolled her eyes and turned her back. "That's the wench who started all of the rumors about me," Ellen whispered to Pearl, who in turn gave Sara his creepiest, most possessed stare.

Seconds later, Sara was obnoxiously booty-bumping Ellen.

"Watch it," Ellen said. Sara looked her eye-to-eye and spilled her red vodka-spiked punch on Ellen's white suede boots.

Ellen looked down at her horrifying, bloodred feet. Her first instinct was to run into the bathroom and cry. But on her way there, she got so pissed off that she wanted to explode. She stood still and got lost in her thoughts while Led Zeppelin blared.

Why the hell am I taking this abuse from a sophomore who thinks that spilling Kool-Aid on someone is clever? For God's sake, she's not even Eve — she's just one of Eve's wanna-bes. And as for Eve, screw her. She's got everything she wants — she's not going to have the satisfaction of making my night a disaster, too. And why do I give a shit if Jack wants a sex-crazed, disloyal ex-best friend? At least it's not me who's falling for it. I DO NOT HAVE TO TAKE THIS.

For the first time, Ellen's emotions raged with anger. She was surprised that she was feeling vengeful instead of pathetic. It had been a long time since she'd tapped into her stubborn feistiness. All of her thoughts and feelings culminated into one brilliant idea.

Ellen decided to fight fire with fire — and it was gonna feel fabulous.

Once the song was over, Ellen sat at the table with Meg and friends, watching for Sara to head to the rest room. Meg and Pearl kept asking Ellen what she was up to, but she totally ignored them. As soon as Sara ran into the bathroom, Ellen sprang up from the table.

"Oh shit," Meg and Pearl said in unison as Ellen sped away.

She ran over to Sara's short, cute freshman boyfriend. She smiled and took his hand.

"Hi," Ellen said. "Wanna dance?"

"Uh, okay," the boy said when he realized that his girlfriend was nowhere in sight. He felt really cool because a junior asked *him* to dance.

Ellen gave him the bump 'n' grind, torturing her poor victim until he could barely keep from undressing her. She was really enjoying this dance. Almost too much, because she nearly missed Sara strutting out of the bathroom with her giggle-addicted girlfriends. That's when Ellen turned she-wolf — this boy didn't stand a chance. She could even smell alcohol on his breath — meaning he was *such* an easy target for Project Seduction. Ellen let her face get closer and closer to his lips until he grabbed the back of her head and kissed her madly. She smooched him back with all the passionate rage she had pinned up inside of her. Just as planned, the kiss ended abruptly when Sara yelled the boy's name. Sara was genuinely traumatized. She tried to look mean as tears flooded her eyes. Ellen smiled wickedly.

Sara ran away with the boy pathetically running after her.

Sara's friends whispered and gave Ellen their bitchiest looks. But she walked away with her chin held high. It felt like the disco ball was spinning just for her. For that moment, *she* was the queen of this dance. She *did* have power. Ellen was so engrossed in her triumph (the first in a looong while) that she barely noticed the music, let alone Meg's cheering or Julian's wide-eyed stare.

Ellen exited the gymnasium just as that old Gloria Gaynor song came on. As she set off for the long walk home, she imagined she had won Best Actress on Oscar night. Her I'm-all-that attitude was the result of sweet revenge. The funny thing was, cruel intentions had never felt so incredibly good before. Then, like finding a long-lost twenty-dollar bill in a jacket pocket, a thought dawned on Ellen: The weight of her problems was lifted. She finally realized that she *would* survive high school.

And she would have her revenge.

CHAPTER ELEVEN

Ellen arrived at her house so emotionally rejuvenated that she almost floated up the stairs to her bedroom. The depression, sadness, and misery were so yesterday to her. Ellen wanted to be a new watch-out kinda woman. She could be a total wench just like anybody else — only smarter. And now was the perfect time to start — Ellen had never felt so powerful in her whole life. The problems that plagued her this morning were no longer issues. Instead, Ellen focused her rage on the issue at hand: revenge. Everyone had wronged her; now she was going to let them know how it felt. Everyone who had hurt her would be begging to kiss her butt freckles soon. Ellen realized that if she could get Sara back without even a thought, she could pull a few genius stunts if she did some serious plotting.

Ellen called it Operation Vindication. And it began the instant Ellen got out her spiral notebook and a pencil. The first name she wrote down was Melisha's.

Operation Vindication
Melisha

The Point: To let her know what it feels like to have something you live for ripped away.

1. *Promote Pregnancy*

Get into her purse, throw away a few of her little green pills, and voilà, *the man-nabber might end up with a baby Jack in her oven. High school as she knows it will be over.*

She pondered if that was just too mean.

2. *Rep Ruination*

What if I post a chart on the Web highlighting every one of Melisha's hook-ups? I bet I could even do a six degrees of sexparation linking her to every guy in Shitville. The URL would look great in the school paper!

3. *Unleash Her Secrets*

For each crush she had — and she had a lot — Melisha wrote down the details of the, um, fineness of each one's bodies. Wonder if she'd like for me to post them on the guys' lockers? Oooh, and what about the one she wrote about our history teacher?!

4. *Drama Downers*

The most important thing to Melisha is that stupid play. Oh, what fun I could have at that play.

5. *Buh-bye, Boyfriend!*

I hate Eve but I bet she could steal Jack. Wonder how much she'd make me pay her?

Eve

The Point: To show my sister that everything can't always turn out her way.

1. *Down with Her Gowns!*

Snip the beads off her competition gowns. After all, she has another beauty pageant in a few months.

2. De-Hair Her

A little peroxide in her Pantene bottle might do her some good.

3. Serves-Her-Right Revenge

Eve keeps a diary, too. Hers might look nice if I put it right next to the kitchen telephone.

4. Mess Up Her Makeup

What if she found her beauty products emptied in the dirty kitty litter box?

5. Hopkins Horror

Ruin her beauty sleep for weeks by haunting her bedroom.

Mr. Cruz

The Point: GET HIM AWAY FROM MY MOTHER!

Um, well.

Huh.

I swear on my life I'll think of something. Or maybe Meg can come up with something.

NOTE TO SELF: CALL MEG ASAP.

Jack

The Point: Humiliate the humiliator — or just cause him heartache in general.

1. Member Mutilation

Bobbit him. (Okay, so I just grossed myself out.)

2. Size Secrets

Speaking of his member, I need to tell the world that he's got a midget.

3. Mom Meanness

Maybe I should just tell him that he's such a jerk, it's no wonder his mom left. Or, ooh, I got it. Meg could call Jack and pretend she's his mother. Meg could persuade him to meet her somewhere, then never show up. That would be brutal.

4. Crush His Coolness

Make everyone realize how lame he really is.

Julian

The Point: Hmmm, he's a hard one. I have no point, I'm just livid because he left me when I needed him most.

1. Sister Sister

Act like Eve on the phone and break up with him.

2. Love-Buster

Plant a note in his locker that says Eve is seeing someone else.

3. Love Lifter

Tell him I'm madly in love with him just to screw with his mind and hurt him like he's hurt me. But I don't really want to do that.

NOTE TO SELF: Go easy on Julian.

The scheming didn't stop when Ellen put her pencil down. Her mind was still whizzing through a thousand new vengeful ideas. Forget feeling sorry for herself, Ellen felt sooo damn good. She couldn't believe how inspired she could be after coming up with a few easy-to-do ideas. Now she just needed a partner in crime . . . and she thought she might have a willing candidate in her mischievous new friend Meg. Anyway, Ellen could feel it — her once-endless days of bawling and brooding were over. From now on, Ellen was all about bravado.

70

She flipped on her TV and an *America's Most Wanted* marathon was on. *This is definitely a sign*, Ellen thought. While studying the plots of the villains, she had fantasies that *she* was on the FBI's most-wanted list. *Ellen Hopkins, sought for the smart-but-sinister revenges on Jack Dillinger, Melisha Smith, Eve Hopkins, Guy Cruz, and Julian Taylor. Please help us stop her before she strikes again. She's sixteen years old, stands at 5'6", and has a nice set of size-C's. Just call . . .*

Oooh, thinking about it felt good — totally soothing and satisfying.

Ellen was on cloud nine (or ten or eleven or twelve), but her revenge-filled rage was beginning to spin out of control.

CHAPTER TWELVE

It was hardly a surprise that Ellen was looking forward to Monday at Shitville High School. It wasn't like her pre-total-disaster days, when she'd get to school early enough to have tons of talk time with Jack, Julian, and Melisha. This time she wanted to see them for different reasons. And finally, she didn't care if anyone whispered, stared, or pointed at her. (Truth be told, the brutal rumors about her were old news. The teenage gossipers were much more fascinated by the two cheerleaders who turned out to be underage exotic dancers.) Nor did she care if she ran into Jack and Melisha making out all over the building. Ellen only concerned herself with one thing: her mission. And that mission made her insanely, acutely happy.

She made up her mind to go for Melisha first. The first part of the plan was to steal her birth control pills. Ellen's heart beat with excitement at the thought of screwing up Melisha's entire life. She envisioned her ex-best friend with pink foam curlers in her hair, working at the Laundromat with a fat, pasty baby on her hip. On the hilarity of that thought, Ellen asked for the hall pass during first period and headed to Melisha's locker —

where the future Maytag maven kept her pill-packed purse. Paranoia and sweatiness set in as Ellen got closer to the locker. Her anxiety worsened when she began fiddling with the lock. She was having second thoughts — it was more fun just *thinking* about the plot. By the time the locker popped open, spitting Melisha's purse onto the floor, Ellen knew that all she was going to do was put it back unmolested.

Then . . .

"Young lady, what do you think you're doing? That's not your locker."

"Uh, I was just looking —" Ellen was really panicky already. As she thought of a hundred excuses, she looked up. Of all the people in this world, Mr. Cruz was the one to catch her pink-handed. Ellen forgot about the fact that she was stealing *and* had originally been trying to see to it that Melisha got pregnant. For the moment, that didn't matter. She was standing face-to-face, again, with *that miserable man*.

"Puh-lease, don't you know this is my best friend's locker? Geez."

"From what I hear, she's not your best friend anymore," he responded coldly.

"Hmmm. Wonder who told you that?" Hate didn't describe how Ellen felt about Mr. Cruz. But she still wished she hadn't made that last catty comment. He might tell Heather that Ellen was catching on to their affair. Oh, she wanted to be the one to confront her mother.

Mr. Cruz was quiet. He scratched his head and said, "Ellen, watch your mouth with me. Actually, you've been quite disappointing lately — antisocial with a terrible attitude."

Who is this guy? He's wrecking a student's home, and he has the nerve to tell me that I have personal problems? Ellen's whole body was beginning to shake with fury. She stood up straight and was about ready to tell him to get the hell off her case. She would have, too, if he had said another word. Instead, she just stared him down.

Then *Guy* stomped off. Ellen wiped her forehead and threw Melisha's purse back in the locker.

What a freakin' failure that was.

Ellen spent the rest of the school day sneaking ciggies, coughing up her lungs, and thinking until her brain hurt. Since the Melisha revenge went so badly, she focused intently on a ruin-Eve daydream. But she abandoned her thoughts when she saw that Julian was strolling down the hall — toward her. He was wearing an oversized blue button-down oxford and a fitted pair of Gap jeans. He slouched a little when he walked — making his tall, lanky body look really cool and, well, sexy. Ellen watched him come closer to her.

Oh my God. I just checked him out. Someone shoot me now. . . .

But she noticed that Julian wasn't smiling. This wasn't a friendly face-to-face.

"What do you want?" she asked — trying to be chilly to compensate for that goo-goo-eyed gaze she just gave him.

"Lose the attitude, Ellen," Julian said. "I heard you were snooping through Melisha's locker today."

Ellen paused because she was surprised anyone knew about that. "Whatever. I don't have to explain anything to you. It's not like you'll take *my* side, anyway."

"That doesn't matter — at lunch I heard Melisha say she still knows your combination. I wanted you to know before you start something that you'll be sorry for. Melisha can be mean."

"*What?!* You're delivering her threats now? Barney scares me more than she does. Anyway, I guess she told you to tell me that."

"*No*, she didn't. You know what? You're impossible," Julian said. "Why did I bother?"

As Julian walked off, Ellen got more and more aggravated. It wasn't her goal to pee in his Cheerios, she just did it accidentally. After he was gone, she realized she could have handled the conversation better. Maybe he *was* just trying to warn her. If he was, she definitely acted out of line, like a total jerk. She was disappointed — she missed him.

Mad, hurt, or whatever she was at Julian, it made her crazy when she realized he was right about one thing: Melisha *could* be mean. Ellen had seen the psycho things Melisha had done to her exes. So she booked it to her locker to make sure her ex-best friend hadn't paid it a little visit. Ellen opened the lock as fast as she could, screwing up the combination on the first try. She opened it and searched through it frantically. At first glance, it looked fine. Ellen began sighing with relief.

As she was about to close it, though, she felt a tremor of terror. Ellen thought she better shuffle through her red backpack to make sure all the important stuff was still there. Sure enough, her calculus *and* biology folders were missing. And of course, Ellen's completed, due-today assignments were in those folders.

THAT BITCH! She steals my boyfriend and my homework? She has to go down.

* * *

Sure, Ellen may have wussed out on the birth control idea, but she wasn't giving up on her other goals of destruction, especially now. Melisha was still going to get it. Sooner rather than later. And Ellen was prepared to take extreme measures — even if it meant that she had to join the drama club. After school, Ellen moseyed over to play practice. She walked right up to the theater teacher, a tall, skinny, wigged-out woman who was addicted to Starbucks and American Spirits.

"Hi, Ms. Jenni. I heard you still need a few stagehands."

"Uh, yeah. We're pretty desperate for some help. The, uh, play is next week! Maybe you can go backstage and — oh, uh, hang on —" She spun around and yelled toward the stage, spilling her stale-java slop along the way. "You need to put more feeling into it, Thomas. Uh, close your eyes and imagine the pain and suffering the character is going through."

"Ms. Jenni, Thomas just left!" another student hollered.

Ms. Jenni rushed toward the stage, leaving Ellen there alone. Luckily, there were no Melisha sightings. Ellen might have lost it on her if she'd seen her. And losing it would spoil the plan.

Ellen walked backstage to offer her services. Then, luck struck for the first time all day. Meg was there painting a balcony prop.

I am so set.

"Hey," Ellen tried to get her attention. "Meg?"

When Ellen looked harder, she could see that Meg was busy drawing Ani DiFranco lyrics on her jeans with permanent markers. When she looked up, Meg was shocked to see Ellen there, too.

"Hey, my woman! You must really need a cigarette bad if you're looking for me here."

76

"Yeah, actually, that sounds good. But I'm really here to be a stagehand."

"You've come to the right place. It's hell painting these backdrops and, of course, no one is helping me. I have to tell you, though — it's more boring than a Barry Manilow concert back here."

"Oh, it won't be one bit dull when we're through."

Meg shared a knowing glance with Ellen, guessing that Ellen had her reasons for being there. And that learning how to paint wasn't one of them.

"Why don't you let me in on what's *really* going on?" Meg said.

"There are a few people in this school who need to be taught very important lessons. I may have been a naive dumbass a month ago, but now I'm sly and out of control. They'll hate themselves for screwing around with me."

"Thank God, girlfriend! I thought you were just going to mope around for the rest of your life."

"That was the old *pathetic* me. Now, I've got big plans. If you're interested, I could use some backup."

"Oh yeah, I hear what you're sayin'. If you don't count me in I'll be offended." Meg certainly wasn't one to miss out on the mischief. She focused intently while Ellen told her the short version of the steamy story between Heather and Mr. Cruz. Ellen thought he might be a good person to start with. Then she mentioned that Mr. Cruz had been picking on her like flies on cow pies.

"He's done — no doubt, girlfriend." Meg's naughty streak wouldn't be wasted on Ellen.

CHAPTER THIRTEEN

"ViVi Star," said the person who picked up the phone.

"Hi, this is Ellen Hopkins." Ellen had made a quick phone call the second she walked in the door. Earlier that year, ViVi and Ellen had totally hit it off. Actually, it was because ViVi, a local Channel Three reporter with a hip wanna-be persona, interviewed Ellen for a story on Generation Y and got super-high ratings. After that, ViVi made it clear that Ellen could call her whenever she wanted.

Ellen figured it was time.

"Ellen? Oh, hi. How are you doing?"

After the plastic pleasantries, Ellen sunk into the meat of her phone call.

"Well, I won't keep you long, but I had an amazing idea for a segment on your newscast," Ellen said.

"Oh, well, do tell." ViVi was a total sham; Ellen had almost forgotten about her phoniness. She tried to make everything sound glamorous — even if she was talking about pig farmers on the outskirts of Shitville.

"Have you heard of my sister, Eve Hopkins? She won the Miss Corncob pageant last weekend, and she'll be going on to compete in the regional Miss Indiana competition in a few months. She's incredibly talented and has an amazing personality."

"Yes?"

"I think she'd be the perfect host of a two-minute teen discussion segment on your newscast every week or so."

"Oh — Ellen! That's chaaahhhrming! You know, we've just been talking about starting one of those."

"Well, I saw that Channel Seven was doing one, so I was hoping I could sell you on the idea of using my sister when you start your own. I think you'll *adore* her. She's brilliant, bubbly, beautiful, and totally in touch with everything teen."

"Oh, I know who she is — she *is* drop-dead. Why don't you send me a tape of her from her pageant, and send me some ideas for how to set up this segment of yours. I think this is fabulous!" ViVi was having visions of the high-profile promotion she might get after her boss heard about this sharp idea.

"You'll have it by Wednesday."

Ellen got off the phone, went home, and got to work. She typed up a ten-page proposal and sent an extra tape of Eve's pageant. Stage One was complete.

Later, about four in the morning, Ellen was shaking with excitement. She wanted to pull a little prank on her bitch sister just to whet her appetite for vengeance. She'd just watched *Nightmare on Elm Street* and thought it might be fun to write "Corncob Queens Must Die" on Eve's bedroom mirror in bloodred lipstick. How terrified would the girliest girl in the world be? Ellen smiled at the thought of it. After all, Eve got nightmares from watching *Scooby-Doo*. A little harmless horror might be all Miss Corncob needed to knock her skyscraper ego down a few notches. And she'd lose a few nights of sleep for sure.

Ellen tiptoed into the bathroom to find the perfect lipstick. Eve's makeup occupied three entire drawers so it took a little while.

That's it. Ellen headed out of the bathroom with a tube that was labeled the color ARTERY.

Eve's bedroom was next. Ellen snuck in and just stood there silently for about three minutes so her eyes could adjust to the dark. Then she made her way to the mirror. She opened the lipstick with the Rob Zombie song "Dragula" playing in her head. Her mind was going "Burn with the witches," just as she drew a C about the size of her hand. Ellen made the slightest *eeee-eee-eeee* noise as the dry lipstick screeched down the mirror.

"ASSHOLE!" The words screeched through the room, and Ellen jumped about five feet when she heard them. At that very instant, she was knocked to the ground. Her heart was pounding so hard it almost exploded. Ellen thought Freddy Krueger was indeed a reality — and he was right there killing her.

But it was just Eve. Ellen was lying flat on her back with her sister's elbow pushed into the delicate dent at the end of her neck.

"Get off of me," Ellen said softly with bloodcurdling meanness.

"I know you hate me, but have you lost your last brain cell? I always knew you were weird, but now you've proven that you're totally psycho, too."

"Get. Off. Me!"

"Fine, then."

Eve shocked Ellen with her next move. She looked her older sister dead in the eye, drew her hand back, and slapped Ellen across the face with her extremely wussy one-hundred-pound might. Then Eve got up and crawled back into bed.

Strangely enough, Ellen lay there half smiling. She was shocked that Eve stood up for herself and didn't go running to Mommy and Daddy. (Ellen was relieved, too — she realized that Heather and Ed would definitely send her to the loony bin for her latest stunt.) As she got up, she realized that she didn't even care if the revenge didn't work. It was just as much fun making Eve incredibly angry.

"Get out of my room. I'm scared of you."

"Oh please, you're the one who's dangerous," Ellen said. "What about planting my diary and getting me in serious trouble? What about stealing my best friend?"

"I only did that after I found out you hated me so much," Eve said. "And as for Julian, you threw him out, anyway. I was just nice to him after you crushed his heart — and, well, we discovered that we had a lot of fun together. That's something *you* don't know how to have."

"You're a sorry excuse for a sister," Ellen said. Then she heaved herself up, walked out of the bedroom, and went to bed. She couldn't sit there and argue over Julian with her sister — that was adding insult to her injuries. And, as for Julian, Ellen was all of a sudden mad at him for getting involved with her archrival sibling.

Whatever, Ellen thought. Eve could say whatever she wanted. Eventually, she'd be paying for everything she'd done.

CHAPTER FOURTEEN

Meg and Ellen made their master plans. While painting backdrops of castles, gardens, and suicide beds, they hashed out the entire thing. Oh, they were going to have a blast demolishing the evil English teacher.

"So, we get the pot plant from your friend Pearl," Ellen said.

"Oh, he and his dad have at least ten, so that is so not a problemo. And Pearl really hates Mr. Cruz. One day, that flaky-ass teacher told the entire classroom that piercing your body was an invasion of your precious, private temple. It was so barfy. Of course, then *Guy* made Pearl go to the front of the room and show off his tongue, eyebrow, and nipple studs to every stiff in AP English. He *killed* Pearl that day. I'm not kidding. Now none of the jocks will pay Pearl to write their papers anymore — and Pearl loved doing that. He used to make so much cash."

"Mr. Cruz is lame, lame, lame. We just need to sneak into his garage. I'm sure my mom has the key — and it won't be hard to swipe her purse for a few hours. Then we place the pot plant there, under a light or something, and leave. For the finale, we call the police and tip them off."

"Let's say he's been selling *ganga* to all the students! I'll testify that he sold some wacky weed to me!"

"Meg, you've never smoked anything harder than a Marlboro Red. And that made you throw up."

"Well, I can pretend I'm the shit-kickin' coolest girl at school if I want to, can't I?"

"What do you mean pretend? We *are* the shit at Shitville High," Ellen said.

"Okay, then, Ellen the Hellion, let's fix your ex, too. We can't just get Mr. Cruz and Melisha. Jack will not escape your wrath."

"He won't. I just haven't thought of anything really, really good yet," Ellen answered.

"I have."

Meg approached Jack while he fished through his locker between second and third periods. As she walked toward him, he honestly didn't notice. When he did see her, it didn't dawn on him that she'd talk to him. Meg was a weird-ass freakin' Coma and not popular at all. She wore lots of black often with mile-high platform shoes. Plus, the girl changed her hair color as much as her underwear. She actually kind of grossed Jack out.

"Hey," Meg said to him.

"Oh, uh, hi, I guess." He didn't even turn to look at her.

"I heard something today that you might be interested in."

"I can already tell you that I'm not. Do you mind? You're interrupting my vibe." He was so sarcastic and cruel with his comment. He hoped she'd run away in tears because she got dissed by *him*. But Meg didn't flinch. And she couldn't care less what this moron said. To her, Jack just proved his disgusting antiwoman pigness. Torturing him would be all the more fun.

"I met your mom the other day."

He was silent on that one.

"I did — she came to the store where I work. She showed me a picture of you." The pain in Jack's face was satisfying enough. Meg just breezily walked away, glowing in the knowledge that her brutal lie would probably keep Jack up at night. Of course, Jack wanted to follow her but he didn't. He wouldn't risk his rep to talk to a Coma — no matter how desperately he wanted to talk to her. And he *was* desperate to talk to her.

Meanwhile, Julian was having a daydream. Sitting in Spanish, he pictured himself with a beautiful faceless girl to cure el boredemo. They were strolling down a street, hand in hand, kissing and hugging and generally snogging.

He ran his hands through her killer hair. He looked at her face — and it was Ellen. *Goddammit. Goddamn her.*

Why didn't I see Eve?

CHAPTER FIFTEEN

"But I want to practice kissing onstage with my *boyfriend*!" Melisha yelled, oblivious to her fellow thespians' suffering. She was pulling rank — as president of drama club and the lead in the play — and acting like a diva. Actually, word in the halls was that Melisha had been a total bitch ever since she had gotten together with Jack. Now she wanted Jack to help her with her "kiss" technique instead of Thomas, the guy who was actually playing Romeo.

Backstage, Meg made Ellen stop slaving away on her English assignment. "Ellen, you *have* to see this."

"But this is the best poem I've ever written," she replied.

Meg pulled her arm. They came in sight of the stage just in time to catch Melisha bitching. Meg was busting a gut at the whole scene while Ellen stayed totally silent. She couldn't help but be disgusted — make that grossed out — by Melisha's display of whiny selfishness and Jack's willingness to be "the man" who knows how to kiss. *Ugh.* She was glad they were with each other; they both deserved torture. *I am so over this,* Ellen thought — and she meant it, too.

"That, uh, [gross throat noise], won't do us any good," Ms.

Jenni announced. She was a nervous wreck — she was just about to kick Melisha right out of the show completely. But, unfortunately, Melisha was good. "I need to see you kiss Thomas. He, uh, you know, Melisha. He's Romeo!"

"But I can't take it — I want to lip-lock my man — then I know I'll be in the right romantic mood to smooch Thomas the way you want me to."

"Uh, oooooh, I need a latte — everybody take five," Ms. Jenni announced as she reached for her empty Styrofoam coffee cup. "I suggest you make out with your boyfriend now if you want to, Melisha. Then I, uh, don't want to hear another word about it." The drama coach's hands were shaking visibly while she walked outside the building.

Meanwhile, Jack burst onto the stage. He, predictably, started being suave and reached around Melisha's waist.

"Give me a smooch like you mean it!" Melisha yelled. "You're *my* main Romeo-man."

With that, he kissed her passionately.

Ellen, watching them from the back of the stage, cringed. Actually, everyone who was watching flinched. This was worse than eating two packets of NutraSweet all at once. They were cheesier than Velveeta.

As they were still kissing, Jack's hand slid down to Melisha's butt.

"Losers," Meg said as she walked back to her paintbrush. She'd been back there painting strands of her now-purple hair with blue paint and humming a Britney Spears song. Yes, Meg was just weird sometimes.

Ellen stood there watching. She tried to stop the feelings from overcoming her. But she missed being kissed like that.

86

Then she started feeling enraged — she saw Melisha glance over at her and kiss him even harder and deeper. Melisha had taken every measure she could to avoid Ellen — and she'd done a pretty good job. But now she was taking a cheap shot.

"Meg, come here a second."

Meg came out, now singing a Limp Bizkit song. "What?"

"They suck."

"Yeah, I agree."

"Let's get 'em. Make them pay."

They discussed the cruel and unusual ways to torment Melisha and Jack on their way to Home Depot in Ellen's Tempo. After that sex scene, play practice was a total downer. Eventually, though, Meg worked her magic on Ellen's mood by changing the entire subject. Meg knew the best dead-baby jokes and then started talking about the kick-ass Ani DiFranco concert that was coming to town. She really wanted Ellen to go with her.

They totally unwound during their twenty-minute drive. When they pulled up to the Home Depot parking lot, they were both disappointed that the ride was over. Ellen rolled up all of the windows, extinguished her Capri, coughed, and turned off the music. Like two mobsters, they coolly strolled inside.

"We need a big pot and some dirt. Where are they?" Meg asked the pimple-plagued salesboy. He pointed them in the right direction, they picked the oldest-looking pot, plunked their cash down, and left.

"You did swipe Mr. Cruz's garage key from your mom, right?"

"Check."

"Pearl's got the pot plant."

"We got the dirt."

"Let's go!"

They picked up the plant at Pearl's house. He walked out of the apartment he lived in with a shorter-than-usual mohawk. Meg told him she dug his new look.

"Thanks, man," Pearl said. "Now let's nail that freak-geek teacher."

They potted the four-foot hemp plant on Pearl's back balcony, then he sent the two girls on their way. Meanwhile, Pearl's dad was dining on some pot brownies. Ellen was tempted to try one, but knew she needed to have a clear mind while she committed her first-ever crime: breaking and entering.

As pumped as Meg and Ellen had been before, they were unusually quiet on their way to Mr. Cruz's house. Somehow, it just didn't feel as festive as it had before. The whole thing made them both nervous as hell, but they didn't dare admit that to each other.

They pulled into his driveway and peeked inside his garage to see if he was home. The coast looked clear.

"Well?" Ellen said as she reached for the key.

"I'll bring the plant." It probably weighed twenty pounds, which was nothing for Meg. She was superpetite but strong — she kick-boxed like a fiend.

"Okay."

They got out of the car and tiptoed around the back of the garage. They went through the door and plunked down the plant. They looked at each other nervously, managed to smile, and got outta there.

Meg hopped in the car and they slid away, stopping in front of a house on the next block. Meg got out her mobile phone to make the Cruz-crushing phone call to the police.

"Uh, Meg," Ellen said. Meg just kept happily pressing the numbers. "Meg . . . MEG!"

"Ellen, what? What? Can't you see I'm busy here?"

"Meg, look straight ahead."

Meg paused, trying to figure out what Ellen was yapping about. "Oh shit!"

Mr. Cruz was trimming his bushes at 137 Regan Street. They had wasted their pot plant by dropping it off at 127 . . . where a station wagon was pulling into the driveway.

"Oh hell, just don't tell Pearl." Meg sighed as Ellen drove away.

"I know I've always encouraged everyone to be accepting of any kind of writing that you encounter," Mr. Cruz said during one of his run-of-the-mill English classes. "But even *I* must trash this piece of, excuse my *français, shit,* that one of your fellow students turned in." He paused and looked around the room. Ellen only looked up from her desk when she felt his eyes burning a hole into the top of her head. She noticed that his long hippie hair needed a cut as bad as a bologna sandwich needs mustard. Plus, his red suspenders looked just plain stupid.

"Now, I'll start with the first line in this poem. . . ."

Mr. Cruz proceeded to critique Ellen's entire piece out loud — the one she had agonized over. What a joke! She knew he was picking on her big-time; her mom and dad told her how great the poem was late last night. Why did he want her to hate him so much?

"I don't want to see such poor use of metaphor, simile, and rhythm. Now that we've had this example, I'm giving everyone's poems back — I want each of you to work on them some more before you turn them in again. Oh, and Ellen, you will not get a chance to redo this poem. You are getting an F."

"What? Everyone else gets another chance," Ellen said while the rest of the class snickered at her misfortune.

"Yes, but I will consider giving you a passing grade if you turn in a four-page essay on the correct way to write a poem. I'd like to see it in two days."

"I'd like to see a lawyer. Is this a fair way to treat your students?"

"My dear, life is not fair."

She couldn't scream, but she wanted to. Ellen would have but she didn't want to risk a trip to the principal's office.

But Ellen's sudden silence didn't mean it would be the last time Mr. Cruz heard from her. This was it — Ellen was going straight to Heather the second she hit the door. *Why should I suffer because my mom is bedding my English teacher? I'm not taking this anymore. She's the one who can deal with him. And she will not be happy when she finds out he trashed my assignment unfairly. I swear I'll beg her to dump this freak. She will, too — or I'll threaten to tell Dad or move out or something.*

That will teach Guy to mess with me.

CHAPTER SIXTEEN

Ellen slammed the door when she got home. She was ready to give her mom the cold, hard facts. She'd been thinking about exactly what to say all day long. She had it all planned out. First, she'd get her mom in the kitchen alone. They'd chitchat, and Ellen would make it simple. She'd say, "I have something to tell you." Ellen couldn't plan what would happen next. And that's the part she was more than nervous about.

"Mom, we need to talk," Ellen said as she walked into the kitchen.

"What do you want to talk about?" The voice wasn't her mother's, it was her dad's.

"Oh, nothing, Dad. Do you know where Mom is?" *Ugh!*

"She'll be back in a few minutes. Are you ready for dinner?"

"Yeah. I'm just going upstairs first."

Where the hell was Heather? If she was at Guy's, Ellen would die. Plus, why wasn't Ed at work — or out teaching some class? He was never home when Ellen arrived after school. So Ellen had to suffer through dinner with her mom, dad, and even Eve. The whole time, she agonized over what she was going to say — and more important, how she was going to get her mother alone so she could say it.

The good thing was, tension had died down at home. If Heather and Ed were mad before, they seemed to have forgiven Ellen. And Heather had stopped acting so detached and strange. It wasn't exactly *Leave It to Beaver*, but it wasn't *The X-Files*, either. And things had been pretty weird there for a while. Basically, though, life was back to normal. Eve pranced around, that was a given. But Heather and Ed had stopped doing those yoga tapes. They seemed to be getting along better, and they even drank Buds every once in a while. At least the mood on the home front would make this conversation a little less excruciating. It was especially good when Ed took off in his Del Sol and Eve went to Sara's. He wanted gourmet coffee.

At last, Ellen had Heather all to herself.

"Mom, we have to talk." Ellen decided to skip the BS and cut to the chase. She was afraid her father would be home quickly, and she'd die if she had to live through another day with butt-crazy Mr. Cruz.

"I agree, we should sit down and talk." That comment sounded like the old Heather, the understanding, I'm-your-friend mom that Ellen was used to.

"Okay, I . . . guess I just have to . . . come out and say this," Ellen said, terrified of the drama she was about to create.

"What, honey?"

"I know all about you and Mr. Cruz."

Heather was silent. She seemed shocked.

"Well?" Ellen said.

"Well, what?"

"Don't lie to me! I've heard your phone conversations.

92

Remember, I was grounded. . . . I was here with nothing else to do but listen twenty-four-seven."

Heather was still silent, which was making Ellen mad. She was expecting an apology from her mom — or an explanation at least.

They sat there uncomfortably for a full minute. Ellen was dying inside because she wanted to finish this up before Ed walked in the door with his java.

"Okay, okay. It's true." Heather was near tears. Ellen was just plain mad.

"I know it's true — how could you?"

"It was a mistake."

"A mistake, huh?" Ellen was saying everything that had been stirring inside her head. *Everything.* She wasn't following the prim-and-proper speech she had prepared so carefully. Instead, she was letting her emotions fly. "Did you know that your *mistake* has been making me miserable for the past month? Did you know that I cringed every time you hugged me and Dad? And what about ripping me to pieces over some alleged thing with my boyfriend while *YOU*, on the other hand, are running around on Dad?"

Heather was trying to hide her tears. But she couldn't. This scene was too painful and embarrassing for her. "I know, Ellen. All of those things are true. I said it was a mistake."

Ellen started to break down, too. She was still angry, but became more emotionally spent than anything. She didn't even realize it at first, but she was crying. "Am I the only one who knows?"

"No," Heather said. "Your father knows."

"Ohmigod. You told Dad?"

93

"I told him — we're working it out, honey. I'm more worried about you."

"Yeah, so worried that you told Mr. Cruz my most private secrets."

"I only told him a little bit," Heather said. "It was going on while you were grounded. It was a bad time for you to be in trouble. I was having a hard time myself."

"Well, your hard time means that Mr. Cruz has been torturing me at school," Ellen said, all worked up again. "I've been getting F's in his class for my straight-A work. He's been busting me in the hallways for things I haven't done."

"You're kidding me." Heather was genuinely surprised. "Has he been doing it lately?"

"Just today. You know that poem I wrote? He gave me an F."

"Oh God, Ellen. I ended things with him for good last week. I can't believe he's acting that way toward you."

"He is. I have no idea what you saw in that freak."

"I just . . . it doesn't matter. It's like I told your father. It was a mistake."

"Yeah, a big mistake," Ellen said, sniffling.

"Ellen, you've made mistakes, too."

"Well, I never slept with Jack."

"I actually kind of figured that out —"

"What?"

"I know you, Ellen, I just know you."

"Well, I don't feel like I know *you*."

"It's going to take a long time to trust me like you used to." Heather suddenly seemed very old. "But I trust you, and I love you. I hope you can trust me again someday soon."

"I hope so, too," Ellen said. *Whoa. This is heavy.* . . . Ellen didn't want to cry again, so she got up from the table. She wished she could talk this over with Julian — he was her only friend who would really understand. But that was a lost cause that became more lost every minute.

Heather got up from the table, too. She reached for a tissue and for her daughter. They hugged awkwardly for a second. "You won't have any more trouble with your teacher. I will at least see to that."

"How?"

"I'll have your father talk to him."

"Oh, man."

"Oh, man is right — like I said, I don't think you'll have any more trouble."

CHAPTER SEVENTEEN

Eve was so clueless. She bounced in the door two hours later and couldn't even tell that Heather was upset. She just started obsessing loudly over her next beauty competition — and it wasn't for six more months. Ellen didn't know how this family would survive without becoming addicted to something. But she forced herself to swallow the sarcasm, walked into the kitchen, and interrupted everybody.

"I have some good news," Ellen announced.

"What? The Comas are coming over for dinner?" Eve remarked.

"You know what? I did something nice for you, and all you want to do is be a bitch."

"Okay, you two," their mother said. "Eve, let Ellen talk."

"I'm sorry." Eve was so fake.

"Well, do you remember when I was on Channel Three last year? And when ViVi Star interviewed me?"

They all nodded yes.

"I called ViVi and asked her if Eve could do a teen talk session on the newscast every once in a while. It turns out they were already looking for the right kid to do it — so I sent them a tape of Eve at her last pageant. And, well, they want her!"

"Are you kidding, Ellen? That was so thoughtful of you!" Heather said, smiling for the first time that night. She hoped this meant her daughters might stop gnawing at each other's throats.

At first, Eve turned pink and started smiling from vain excitement. But then she realized that her sister was up to something. Why would Ellen, who was trying to terrify her in the middle of the night, do *anything* decent for her? Eve sure as hell hadn't tried to be cool to her older sister — Eve took pride in flaunting her happy relationship with Julian as much as she could around Ellen.

"Ellen, what's the catch?" Eve asked, much to the shock of her parents. They thought Eve would be pee-her-pants pleased.

"Eve! You should be thanking Ellen. This is a really big deal," their father said.

Eve still didn't believe it, but she decided to play along.

"You're right," Eve said. "I really am excited, just a little bit surprised."

"Well, don't be. This is like my congratulations gift to you, Eve." Ellen was finessing this scene with perfect calculation — it was going exactly as planned. "Really."

Ellen grabbed her black ponytail holder and put it around her wrist as she rushed out the door for school. Meg was sitting in the driveway, fingering through her back-to-blond hair. She kept beeping the horn of her 1980s-style Pinto — she had painted the car pink herself.

"Hey, Ellen — you look like a star today, homegirl. What the hell is up?"

"I told you, I'm a new me," Ellen said. She was still wearing a black tank top and khaki cargo pants — her style hadn't changed. It was the sparkle in Ellen's eye that made her look more beautiful than ever. Finally, things were going *her* way.

"No doubt," Meg said as she passed Ellen a cigarette. "Are you ready for today's assignments?"

"I can't wait."

They arrived at school about an hour before anyone else got there. They went straight to the newspaper office, where they could use the free copy machine. They made five duplicates of the juiciest note that Melisha had ever written to Ellen. Today, that note was going public.

Meg and Ellen taped a note to Melisha's locker, Jack's locker, the common area where everyone hung before class, Ms. Jenni's classroom door, and in the lunchroom. Pretty soon, all of Shitville High would know that Melisha had a hot, lusty crush on their history teacher — and that she planned to seduce him to get an A in the class. It was written in Melisha's own handwriting, with her name signed below. (Luckily, Melisha hadn't written "Ellen" or "E —" anywhere on the note.)

They sat down in the common area and watched the students read their posters before they went to class. Eventually, a teacher came and took it down. But that was fine — the damage had been done. The gossip machine was purring like a panther.

"Let's see her take my homework assignments again," Ellen said.

"Not to mention your boyfriend!" Meg replied.

Meg ran to class feeling one hundred percent grrreat. She was good at helping people out of toughies — but she'd never met someone like Ellen before. Ellen's life really sucked. It made Meg happy to think she was helping someone come back from the dead.

The bell rang while Meg was at her locker. *Late again*, she thought. She stopped rushing around — heck, she was already tardy. While she reapplied her mascara in her locker mirror, she heard a *"PSSST."*

Meg whipped her head around but saw nothing.

"PSSST. Over here." The noise was coming from the nearby boys' bathroom. She smiled, thinking Pearl was just being silly again. She walked into the rest room to chat with him. Only it wasn't him — it was Jack.

"Hi, uh, Meg." His head was down, his hands in his pockets. He was looking around nervously. He didn't want to be seen talking to *her.*

"What do you want?"

"I, um . . . I really want to know where you saw my mother. I mean, I would pay you or do whatever you want."

"Whatever I want?"

"Uh, yeah, baby." Jack was always the womanizer. He'd be flirty with a weird chick — well, as long as no one found out about it.

"I don't know what I want for that information. Let me think about it."

"Come on."

Meg gave him a bitchy look and walked out. She smiled as soon as she turned her back. *How pathetic that guy is.*

Ellen was feeling totally gratified at play practice. Melisha spent most of the rehearsal in tears — kids were ruthless in their teasing. Not only that, word was that she'd been called to the guidance counselor's office to "talk" about her feelings.

HAHAHAHAHAHAHA! Ellen couldn't have been happier. Until her good mood was crushed later that day.

Ellen was enjoying the silence of the house when the phone cut her thoughts short.

"Hello," Ellen said, expecting someone to try to sell weed killer or something.

"Oh, hey, honey, I thought you were out with Sara." The voice was unmistakably Julian's. Eve *was* out with Sara, but Julian thought he was talking to her — so Ellen just let him go on thinking it.

"Uh, no, Sara decided she didn't want to go," Ellen said slyly.

"I was hoping I'd catch you."

"You did. What's up?"

"I just had your sister on my mind. I just finished my college application and all —"

"My sister? Why were you thinking about her?"

"I know she's your favorite subject to trash and all, and you know I don't like to talk about her — but I'm so shocked by what she did to Melisha today. I remember when Melisha wrote that note. This whole thing really bothers me." Two things surprised Ellen during this conversation. First of all, she didn't think Eve wasted a minute of her precious time talking about her. Second, why would Julian still concern himself with anything Ellen did? It's not like he bothered speaking to her.

"Yeah, it was heinous, huh?"

"It *was* heinous. I know she's had a tough time lately. But she's not the girl I used to be best friends with. You know? No matter what Melisha did, my Ellen would never go after her like that."

"Uh, don't be so sure." Ellen tried to sound cool like Eve would.

"Promise you won't get mad at me, but I miss Ellen so much. The old Ellen, that is."

"I miss —" Ellen caught herself before she blew her cover. She was so happy to hear those words. She thought he'd forgotten all about her, and here he was, missing her. It was wonderful!

"What?"

"Oh, I was talking to Mom. . . . Anyway, I was saying, live here, then you'll get all of her you can handle," Ellen said. It was hard to gauge what Eve would really say — it's not like they ever chatted.

"Yeah, well. She has ruined herself completely. I don't think I'll ever talk to her again. She's, like, insane. She's mean, crazy, and cruel. I never thought I could ever hate her." *What?!!! I thought he just said he missed me.*

"You don't really hate her." Ellen would rather go through all of her recent heartaches three times over than to hear that Julian really hated her. But the fact that he'd say that to Eve really enraged her. *Ruined myself? You're the one who's dating Eve! That's ruining yourself.*

101

"I think so."

Ellen made up a dumb excuse and ended the conversation. She was hurt — more so than she wanted to be — by his biting, honest words. She was almost aware that what he said was probably right. But she was too mad to get in touch with her feelings. She just wanted to get him, too. He was kissing evil Eve *and* dissing Ellen. Julian had hurt his Elle much more deeply than he ever would have guessed. And the only way Ellen could deal was to get revenge.

Ellen woke up way too early the next morning. She called up Meg.

"Are you on crack, Ellen? What time is it?"

"Oh, it's about six. Hey, come get me, 'kay?"

"I am not coming over there before the sun rises."

"It's worth it. . . ."

"Ellen the Hellion, huh? I'll be there in an hour or so."

With that, Ellen hopped in the shower and got ready for another day at Shitville High. She just had to make a quick stop before she hit school. When Meg finally arrived, Ellen explained everything. Meg agreed, but she wasn't into it.

"I just don't feel your plan, man," Meg said as she fiddled with her Bob Dylan CDs. "Maybe we should save all of our energy for the play debut on Saturday."

"Nah, this will only take a second."

Meg drove to Julian's house with about as much enthusiasm as a passed-out drunk. She didn't offer Ellen a cigarette, saying she'd given them up completely for Gobstoppers. She didn't even turn up her car stereo as she pulled up next to the mailbox. Ellen failed to notice Meg as she opened the box and reached inside to take the prize she was after — Julian's application to Harvard. She took it just as Meg peeled away.

Ellen ripped it into a hundred tiny pieces and threw it out the Pinto window. Meg was still silent. Ellen's heart was heavy — she felt like a naughty child. Like when she was five and ate a piece of Eve's birthday cake before her party started.

Maybe it wasn't cool, Ellen thought. *But my mission was accomplished.*

And that was all that mattered.

"Ellen, that wasn't cool." Meg had to say it. She couldn't be silent on this one. Ellen suddenly felt guilty. Very, very guilty.

CHAPTER EIGHTEEN

The school day sucked. First of all, Ellen's locker was totally empty. Everything had been taken out. It had to be Melisha. She was the only one who would be lame and uncreative enough to pull the same stunt twice. Ellen was annoyed — Melisha took her cool posters down, stole her neato Hello Kitty mirror, thieved all of the textbooks, and took her Barenaked Ladies CD. It was a pain in the ass — but Ellen had expected it. She had put her folders and homework in Meg's locker and was going to take the rest of her stuff over there soon. Melisha just beat her to the punch.

And it didn't help that Ellen kept seeing Julian in the hall, looking all tired. She figured he'd been up all night perfecting that application. She wanted to run up to him and fess up. She couldn't do it, though. He'd hate her beyond belief. But Ellen knew that she deserved the wrath of Satan for what she had done. *Why did I do that? I think I am going crazy.*

Her spirits lifted later that day when Meg gave her some good gossipy news.

"Melisha has some competition," Meg said.

"I hate her."

"Just listen. I thought Jack was following me out to the track where we smoke sometimes —"

"He what?"

"You know, he's trying to get me to tell him what I know about his mother. Which is nothing but . . ."

"Oh, yeah," Ellen said. "Then what?"

"Well, it turns out that he wasn't following me. Some freshman girl met him out there, and they started going at it."

"No way!"

"Yes way, girlfriend. I'm not kiddin'!"

"God, he's gross. I'm lucky I didn't catch cooties from him."

"You know what?" Meg asked. "I think we need to plot a mega-major revenge against him. This mother stuff is silly."

"Oh, girl," Ellen said, "I do agree."

Ellen was delighted to go to play practice. Not because she could look at Melisha and know something that she didn't know, but because she was carrying out her ultimate revenge plan. She and Meg were going to pummel some of the play props, the ones they'd worked so hard to create. Meg thought it would be hilarious if the castle had rap-inspired graffiti on it. Or if Juliet's bedroom turned out to be fluorescent green. So after everyone left the big rehearsal on Friday night, Meg and Ellen stayed. They waited until everyone left — which took forever — and got to work.

Meg had the green, purple, orange, and yellow paint all ready. She was going to town. Ellen was just there to help and take orders. After all, it was Meg who was the artist.

With one spray paint can in each hand, Meg stood before the castle she'd been slaving over for the last two months. She started to squirt the letters DMX in orange paint, then stopped. Meg put the paint cans on the ground, then she sat down, looking at her stage-sized castle.

"Okay, what's going on here? Don't we have some mass destruction to get to?"

"I can't do it. I can't."

"Shit, Meg."

"These props are my ticket to a good art school in a year. I need to save these for a while, photograph them, and put them in my portfolio. I mean, look at them — I don't mind if I say so my goddamn self. I did a kick-ass job."

Ellen had to admit that the props were artistic. They were better than anything the school had used before. When Ellen actually took a moment to study the details of the tables, rooms, balcony, and castle that Meg had created, she was incredibly impressed.

"You're right, Meg. These are brilliant. Let's go home."

Disappointment weighed heavily on their minds. Meg and Ellen really wanted to see Melisha give birth to a hippopotamus tomorrow when she saw that her precious play was ruined.

But instead, it looked like the show would go on.

Ellen wracked her brain all night to figure out what she could still do to get Melisha. After screwing with her locker again, that girl had to go down. Ellen, once again, found herself drawn to the bathroom. Her last trick on Eve — tampering with zit cream — had worked wonders. Eve's complexion was suffering. So Ellen tried to think of something medicinal she could pull on Melisha.

She was drawn to the Ex-Lax gel tabs. The label read: *Guaranteed to loosen you up in just one hour. Just imagine — what if Melisha "accidentally" took a couple of these during our preshow party tomorrow. About forty-five minutes before her debut as Juliet . . . Oh, how glorious thou shalt be!*

The household pack of bowel-movers wasn't even opened. There were twenty tablets just for Melisha's taking. And Ellen had already volunteered to bring refreshments to the preshow party tomorrow night.

The Ex-Lax pills had been all pulled apart. Now they were reduced to a few tablespoons of powder that Ellen kept in a Ziploc bag. She got out a recipe for some delicious ice-cream punch — carbonation and dairy products were sure to aggravate Melisha's Ex-Laxed digestive system.

Ellen made two batches — one with a little bag full of little white powder added to it. And one that was left untampered with. After all, a lot of people in the play had become Ellen's friends — she didn't want to induce diarrhea in everybody.

She sealed the Tupperware tops of both punch containers, got in her Tempo, and headed to the high school auditorium. She was running late, so she was sure all the kids would be waiting for her.

Meg saw Ellen walk in first.

"I'm, like, thirstier than a fish in the desert. Gimmee some of that great-looking stuff. Did you spike one of them with vodka, 'cause I could sure use a drink?"

Ellen hadn't told Meg about the plan simply because she hadn't had time. She just thought of it at midnight last night!

"Oh, um, let me get it for you. There's no vodka in it, though." Ellen grabbed the cups and poured a glass full of Ex-Lax-less punch.

"Bummer." Meg took her glass and headed off to the set. She was having trouble getting the balcony to stand up straight. "Thanks, man."

Ellen got so nervous at the prospect of the fiasco she was about to create. It was exciting but just plain gross. And she imagined that if she was caught, she'd, like, have to switch schools or something. Or maybe her parents would commit her to the loony bin. She also thought about Meg. For the first time ever, Meg was a part of something she enjoyed. Ellen hated to ruin it for her.

It wasn't brain surgery — Ellen reluctantly decided to serve the nonspiked punch. She walked back to the bathroom and flushed the contents of the other container down the toilet. She was only gone five seconds, but when she got back, her punch was all gone. Melisha had two full cups in her hands.

Feeling a little beaten, Ellen took the empty container to the bathroom to rinse it out. She noticed that the Tupperware had a weird, white powdery film around it. Ellen's heart skipped a beat.

Ooooooooooops. Well, well, this will be an interesting evening after all.

The real drama took place about thirty minutes into the play. Just when Romeo, AKA Thomas Buttorf, was reciting his beautiful lines of love to Juliet, AKA Melisha the Monster, the Ex-Lax made its move.

"He jests at the scars that never felt a wound . . . ," Thomas said.

"But soft! What light through yonder window breaks?
It is the east, and Juliet is the sun!"

Peering from backstage, Ellen's eyes were glued to Melisha. Talk about a green face — Melisha's was the shade of a toad while Thomas continued.

"Arise, fair sun, and kill the envious moon,
Who is already sick and pale with grief."

That line made Ellen laugh out loud. The other stagehands looked at her like she was loony.

Thomas looked healthy and must have escaped the poopy punch.

"That thou her maid are more fair than she.
Be not her maid, since she is envious;
Her vestal livery is but sick and green."

Just then, Ellen — along with the other four hundred people who were watching — heard a squish-squish noise coming from Melisha's microphone. It sounded just like a wet, juicy fart.

But who knows? Sometimes those mikes play mean tricks. So the show went on for a few more minutes. But Mercutio was having the same audible squish-squish problem just as foul odors wafted from the stage. A few minutes later, two characters who were supposed to go on next raced to the bathroom with terror in their eyes. They didn't come back.

But Melisha was in worse shape. She was still out in front of the most popular kids and their parents. She thought she could handle the urgency in her colon. She squeezed her

sphincter tight as she recited her lines. But there was no holding back — Melisha's mouth went silent. Her other body parts
did the talking. A runny brown blob oozed out of Melisha's
exquisite, bright-red Juliet gown and landed on the floor of the
stage. The audience members in the first row winced. She ran
offstage in tears and hurried toward the bathroom.

The bulky kid who played Mercutio followed her — he was
in dire need of the rest room himself.

The whole place fell silent. A few seconds later, giggles
came from the back of the auditorium. That's where the Comas
were sitting.

Ms. Jenni yelled for Ellen to lower the curtain immediately.
That night, the show was canceled.

Melisha spent an entire hour in the bathroom. When she
finally emerged, she had poop stains all over the back of her
costume.

Filled with the energy of spitefulness, Ellen pulled one more
prank that night. She spiked her sister's Pantene bottle with a
quarter cup of peroxide. A fried head of hair would look nice
along with Eve's tomato-y complexion — especially since ViVi
Star was all set to tape Eve's new teen segment on Monday.

CHAPTER NINETEEN

The post-weekend gossip at Shitville High School had never been so outrageously, gloriously raunchy. No one could stop talking about how the school show was ruined because the characters pooped themselves midplay. Not surprisingly, Melisha skipped — still feigning deathly stomach illness that Ellen knew was fake. Jack was absent, too — he was so hypersensitive to embarrassment that he couldn't even handle it when it was his girlfriend's.

Ellen considered herself a genius. Between posting the note about bonking the history teacher and kick-starting a certain thespian's bowel movements (even if it was by accident), Ellen had effectively destroyed Melisha's rep. It was so demolished that it was definitely beyond repair. Ellen took pleasure in knowing that now Melisha knew exactly how that felt.

Yes, it was a great day for Ellen. First of all, Meg was so cool. She never said anything to Ellen about the dramatic *Romeo and Juliet* debacle. But despite all of the peroxide fumes Meg had encountered due to hundreds of hair color changes, she was still supersharp. She somehow knew Ellen was behind the whole thing. And she had great admiration for her new friend —

her first close buddy who wasn't a Coma *or* a big fan of Barfing Spaghetti.

Secondly, Mr. Cruz gave Ellen his gold star of approval on her latest assignment. He didn't speak to or look at her ever, but that made Ellen pleased as, well, punch. She had come face-to-face with him in the hallway a few days before. She just smiled and asked him in her most sarcastic way how he was doing. He put his head down and walked on by. As he did, Ellen called him a sleazeball under her breath. She wanted to be mean to him — and she was. But regardless of the rift between them, Ellen was again getting good grades. *Heather — or Ed — must have really set Guy straight. I don't care how, I'm just glad they did it so I didn't have to. I'm getting out of the Ex-Lax-slipping business. Well, soon, anyway.*

After school, Ellen, Meg, and the homecoming-queen crowd went back to the auditorium. This time they were there to see another show. Eve the beauty queen was taping her first segment of *The Teen Scene Live* on Channel Three. Ellen spotted Julian in the crowd — he was sitting next to Sara, looking uncomfortable. Ellen thought about his trashed application again. She had been meaning to fess up and tell him — after all, she didn't want to ruin his life. Ugh. She'd do it later. At the moment, she had other things to think about.

She knew her execute-Eve plan was moving right along schedule because she heard a few pom-pom girls whispering about how skanky Eve Hopkins looked.

"Talk about a bizarro hair and skin day!" one of them said with envious delight.

But the real fun was just starting. ViVi Star was sitting with

112

Eve, giving her last-minute tips on how to be the perfect on-screen hostess. Eve was all set to get student reaction about teen sex in the new millennium. She had to ask a few students if they were currently doing it — it was part of a ratings scheme on Channel Three. Eve was noticeably nervous — she didn't know much about intercourse that wasn't a requirement of her cock-teasing specialty. But she was excited to be on television regardless. She'd been going on about her future as an MTV VJ lately if everything went well on *The Teen Scene Live.*"

Eve's big moment arrived — ViVi and the Channel Three camera crew shushed the audience, then gave Eve and Shitville High a cheesy introduction.

"And now to Eve Hopkins, our sixteen-year-old Teen Scene Queen," ViVi said.

"Thanks, ViVi. We're here today at a local high school to talk about everyone's favorite subject — sex. Teenage pregnancy is on the decline nationwide, but that doesn't mean that kids have stopped having sex."

So far, all was going well.

"Next, we'll ask a few young people about their own personal sexual experiences. What you may learn will shock you."

"First, how many of you are having sex?" Eve asked as the camera panned the audience. About a third of the students raised their hands. Then someone yelled, "I only do it with you, hotness!" from the back row.

Eve laughed nervously at that comment and kept going. "Now I'm going to ask Randall Jillson to come up here and —"

Just then, some loudmouth yelled, "Eve eats it!"

Eve did a ten-second interview with Randall before ViVi took over and began to sign off. Just then, Pearl ran across the stage wearing nothing but a green thong. His mohawk was greener and higher than usual, and he had the words "Beauty Queen Eat Me" painted on his bulging stomach. He paused long enough for the camera to catch a shot of him, then ran out the door behind the stage before anyone had a chance to catch him.

And that was the end of the show.

Ellen laughed until her sides split. Meg had mascara — and one fake eyelash — dripping down her cheeks. It was Meg's job to hand out the twenty-dollar bills to the two boys who helped make a mockery out of Eve's news segment.

Eve smiled and stayed cool as always, but Ellen could tell she was mortified. ViVi and Channel Three left. No one came to the stage to congratulate her, so Eve headed out the door.

The wailing was unmistakable. Ellen could hear it before she walked through the front door. Eve was apparently unhappy with her *Teen Scene* show.

From what Ellen could make of the conversation, ViVi had called and said thanks for everything but Channel Three wouldn't be needing Eve's services any longer. They needed a teen who was more "relatable" to their audience.

"You looked great and had a new, exciting experience. Isn't that all that matters, anyway?" Heather said as she hugged her.

"Actually, those kids were pretty funny, Eve. At least you made everyone at school laugh," her father said.

"Ed, you're not helping," Heather said to her husband.

"But Mom," Eve sniffled. "They're not going to let me go on television anymore. My whole career is ruined — I'll never be on MTV now! And what if the judges of the next pageant saw that? Oh, this is awful."

Their dad left the room because he couldn't keep from laughing.

Eve's crying slowed down. It was now a whimper.

Heather looked up at Ellen with a strained smile. Ellen walked over and put her hand on Eve's shoulder. "I'm *so sorry* that this happened, Eve."

Her sister's reply was a teary, pathetic "thanks." She hung her chin low and headed to Sara's for a cheer-up.

Oh shit, I'm a monster, Ellen thought. *I've definitely gone past sane limits. Did I take this one too far? She is my sister, even if I do hate her. Maybe I should tell her that Channel Three won't be airing her tape. That's what ViVi told me today.*

Ellen picked up the phone when it rang, thinking it would be Meg wanting to have another good giggle over their most recent prank.

"Hi." Well, it wasn't Meg. The voice on the line was as familiar to Ellen as an old, soft pillow — too bad the sound of it had come to create pangs of tension and panic.

"Uh, hi," Ellen said. She was speaking to none other than Melisha the Original Monster, the girl who pooped in her pants and skipped school. At least this time Ellen got a sense of satisfaction from dealing with MOM. But that didn't mean she felt totally comfortable and confident about the call. She was nervous because Melisha was sure to rip her up. She was furious because — after all this time — this annoying witch had the nerve to call. Ellen was so livid at Melisha for everything she'd done that the heat of her skin could have barbecued a chicken breast.

Ellen was a mess because she hated Melisha but remembered how much she had once loved her.

"You are a crazy bitch," Melisha said. With that sentence, Ellen was relieved. At least defensiveness and anger were the only feelings she'd need to show. It was much easier to just be plain furious, instead of riding the emotional roller coaster of pure hurt and vulnerability.

"Look who's talking. Didn't you used to be my best friend?" Ellen spewed. She worked herself into a real fury. She let her biting words and outrageous rage rip. "You know, before you had sex with my boyfriend?"

"I didn't drug the stars of a play."

"Well, neither did I," Ellen lied without feeling one bit bad about it. Melisha deserved everything she got. Times a thousand.

"Oh puh-lease. Just like you didn't post my private notes all over Shitville."

"You're a bitch, and you deserved it," Ellen fessed up, also without feeling one bit bad about it. She was in the mood to sink to lower and lower levels just to verbally abuse Melisha.

"You're crazy, and you're a freak."

"You've always been a freak," Ellen said. Now, since she finally had the chance to ask, she drilled Melisha. She knew her ex used to hate to be put on the spot. So that's exactly what Ellen did to her. "If we were ever real friends, how could you possibly do everything you did to me?"

"What can I say? I did what I did." That was a typical, noncommittal Melisha answer. It was the kind of answer that always drove Ellen insane.

"Yeah, well, you were a bitch." She realized her comeback was lame. She was mad as hell, and her fury was muting her most clever brain cells.

"Okay, fine, we're both bitches, Ellen." Melisha was trying to get to the point so she could get off the phone.

Ellen was trying to pick a fight. "No. I just gave you what you had coming." Mad or not, she couldn't help thinking how weird it was to be treating Melisha this way. If a psychic had told her a year ago all of this would happen, she never in a million years would have believed it. But there she was in that situation. It was not a fun place to be.

"Shut up for a second, I didn't call you for fun."

"I just wish you hadn't called."

"Listen," Melisha said. "This has to end."

"You started it. I think I can decide when it's over."

That's when the inevitable started to happen. Melisha sounded like she might cry. Ellen wouldn't have admitted it, but Melisha's tears always had the power to soften her. Not that Ellen was going to melt into a pool of warm butter. But as much as she didn't like it, Ellen wasn't immune to Melisha's emotions. They had been friends for too long for Ellen to remain totally unaffected.

"Please, then, tell me it's over. I can't take this anymore. I have enough to worry about. Nothing is going right." She was definitely crying by this time. Then the lightbulb flickered in Ellen's head — the whole reason for this call could be because something bad happened between Melisha and Jack. She sure hoped so.

"I don't care what you can and can't take. I'm sick of you." Ellen meant that with all of her heart. She tried to ignore the sobbing. Within about a minute it stopped, and Melisha got catty.

"Look, if you don't stop going after me, then I'll keep going after you. Can we just agree to hate each other and leave it at that?"

That was the most intelligent thing that had come out of Melisha's mouth in months. Ellen didn't want to keep thinking up new ways to be mean to her. She didn't want to think about Melisha anymore at all. So Ellen replied,"I will on one condition."

"What?"

"That you help me with something."

CHAPTER TWENTY

Play practice was over, so Meg and Ellen were a little bored after school lately. Meg thought it would be a good idea if Ellen gave her old friend Melisha a call.

"Hey, it's Ellen."

"Hi."

"I noticed you weren't in school today."

"I won't be in school all week. Would you go after you shit your pants in front of four hundred people *and* when the school thinks you're a ho-bag, history-teacher seductress? I so don't think so. I'm not lettin' the lions eat me alive while I'm standin' right there. They can do it while I'm at home watching *Jerry Springer*," Melisha explained.

"Listen, I know you're not sick, so come over."

"I really don't feel like it."

"Guess what I'm holding right now? A note you wrote that says you want to boink Bump."

"God, Ellen! I guess I'll be right there."

When Melisha arrived, she could see Meg and Ellen hanging out Ellen's window smoking cigarettes. Just like old times, Ellen had a can of Glade in her free hand.

After they said cold hellos, Ellen got down to business.

"I need you to help me get Jack," she said.

"I —"

"I don't care what you say, Melisha. You owe me big-time, and after you hear what I have to say —"

"I already know. You're going to tell me he's cheating on me, right?"

"With that freshman cheerleader."

"Yeah, the bitch."

"What are you talking about?" Ellen yelled. "She doesn't know you. *You* were my friend for the last sixteen years. You have no idea what it feels like."

"Do you want me to say I'm sorry, Ellen? Will that make it better? I'm sorry, okay? I chose Jack and, obviously, it was a dumb choice. What else do you want me to say?"

"I wanted you to say you were sorry a long time ago, not flaunt around in front of me. Not desert me when I had *no* friends."

"Well, I'm the one with no friends now," Melisha said, all whiny.

It made Ellen cringe. She couldn't care less.

"Will you two stop it," Meg broke in. "Hate each other all you want, just help each other get Jack."

"Fine."

"Fine."

Ellen explained the plan that she and Meg had master-minded. It involved sex, lies, and seduction. The three girls loved it.

*   *   *

Later that night, Ellen was full of mischief and fun. That's why she called Julian's house and hung up — twice. But much to her surprise, Julian called her back. He surprised Ellen because he never had Caller ID when they were friends.

"Eve, I know that's you."

Thinking fast, Ellen pretended to be her sister once again. "Yeah, Julian?"

"I thought we talked about this. . . ."

"Oh, we did?" *I'm slicker than a VO5 hot oil treatment*, Ellen thought.

"Yes, we *did*. We decided not to talk to each other for a while." *Broken up? What? No way! Eve didn't let on about this.*

"I know. I miss you, though," Ellen, AKA Eve, said.

"I hope you're still not super-upset. I feel bad that I've hurt you."

Eve hurt? That's a new one, Ellen thought.

"But I told you," Julian explained. "I've tried my hardest but I'm still hung up on Ellen. I can't get her out of my head. She's so damn stubborn and unique. It's just something about that girl. I have to give her one last chance."

Ellen heard words she'd been dreaming about lately. It felt so funny, but she had developed an unreal crush on Julian. She thought about him all the time. She dreamed about their conversations and their first kiss. She kicked herself for not taking advantage of what she had when he was around.

Ellen was so stunned by his words that she couldn't say anything else. She slammed down the phone and her heart beat like a blender grinding up frozen strawberries. Julian still cared about her? *What the hell?* She was wildly excited at the

121

news. It was more exciting than when she first started dating Jack.

But then she remembered something that made her almost cry. She had cruelly ripped up Julian's Harvard application. For the first time since Ellen's "I Will Survive" moment on the school dance floor — when she kissed Sara's dorky dude — she thought revenge sucked. It was fun at first because the line between right and wrong had seemed blurry. But once the buzz of revenge wore off, Ellen was stuck with herself. The right/wrong line was suddenly much clearer. She knew some of what she'd done was wrong — but what she'd done to Julian was unforgivable. Or maybe it wasn't — she hoped he would forgive her.

After a day of agonizing at school, Ellen finally forced herself to go to Julian's house. She did it partly because Meg kept hounding her to fess up about the whole Harvard application thing. Then there was That. Phone. Conversation. Ellen's emotions were all mixed up. Only one thing was for sure: She had to tell Julian the truth — about the application, that is. The other stuff? She preferred to keep it bottled up.

Ellen stood at the door, looking beyond beautiful in a gray tank top and a zip-up black jacket. Her shiny hair had grown — it rested on Ellen's gorgeous womanly body. Julian was overcome with emotion at the mere sight of *Elle*.

But Ellen felt freaked-out weird. She felt Julian's eyes pierce through her. She sensed that she had just been checked out.

"Hey," Ellen said.

"Hi, Elle." The way Julian said that made Ellen tingle.

"Can we talk?"

"I'd really like that," Julian replied. Sure, he was mad at her for being so mean, but overwhelmed by her, too. He truly hoped there was another side of the story that would vindicate Ellen in his eyes.

It seemed like a hundred years since these former best friends had spoken. Really, it had only been a couple of weeks. But Julian told Ellen all about his breakup with Eve. Ellen told Julian all about her bonding with Meg. After about an hour, Julian and Ellen went inside to dine on some Phish Food. As they walked in the front door, Julian touched the small part of Ellen's back. She couldn't get over how blue his eyes looked that day.

As she scraped, scraped, scraped her ice-cream bowl clean, Ellen said, "Julian, there's something I have to tell you."

His eyes widened, and he smiled. "There's something I have to tell you, too."

"Um, let me go first." Ellen paused for five full seconds. "You know your Harvard application?"

"How did you know about that?"

"Uh, from my, uh, sister," Ellen said. "But that's not what's important. I, um, found it and threw it away."

Julian just looked down at his melty last spoonful of Phish Food. He said nothing. He felt like dying inside from disappointment. Not really because of Harvard — but because this girl he had put on a pedestal always seemed to fall off it and crush him.

"But I wanted to fess up and tell you. I was crazy with jealousy over you and Eve. And Eve was rubbing it in my face every chance she got. And I, and I, you know. I went crazy."

"You did go crazy."

123

"Julian, I am so sorry," Ellen said as she reached over to touch Julian's hand.

Julian pulled it away and put it between his knees. He looked beaten and abused.

Ohmi-holy-god. What have I done? Who have I become?

"Ellen, I'm going to try to keep calm," Julian said, now thinking about the consequences of what his friend had done. He became angry — she knew how important that application was to him.

Speaking is good . . . at least he's talking to me, Ellen thought.

"But I . . . I." Julian stopped.

"I'll help you do another one. You don't know how awful I feel."

"Screw calm," Julian said. The more he thought about it, the more rip-shit he got. "How could you do that to anybody? Especially to me? Have you lost your mind? What the hell is wrong with you?"

"I'm sorry," she said as she reached for his shoulder. He stepped back as she said, "That's why I'm here explaining this to you. I can't tell you how bad I feel."

"I don't think I know you at all." Julian paced. "You've changed too much for me." He didn't know if that fact hurt him or her more, but he didn't let her know that.

She could tell he was about to kick her out. "Come on, Julian, let's talk about this."

"I'm done talking. I can't stand the sight of you right now."

Ellen got up and ran out the door — she didn't want Julian to see her upset.

Julian cared about her more than he cared about himself; he

124

knew that. It didn't matter what she did to him. He just wished she would stop disappointing him. He shook his head, wiped his eyes, and sat down. *She'll never stop breaking my heart.* He sat there for almost an hour.

Finally, Julian went into his room and put on his Barenaked Ladies CD. He turned up "Old Apartment" as he reprinted out his entire Harvard application. At least he still had plenty of time to resend it. But he wasn't going to tell Ellen that.

CHAPTER TWENTY-ONE

Melisha was messing around with her answering machine. She called Ellen to test it out.

"Ellen, say something."

"Something."

"C'mon, more than *that*, sweetie tweetie."

"Melisha, don't bother me now. I'd rather dunk my breasts in boiling water than talk to you."

"Perfect! Hold on a second." Faintly, Ellen could hear Melisha fiddling around with something. Then she heard her voice.

"It's working!" Melisha announced.

"Great. Can I go now?"

"Yep!" Melisha was in way too good a mood for Ellen.

Anyway, Melisha had more important things to do than talk to Ellen — she had to call up Jack. She only called Ellen to make sure she could tape phone conversations with her answering machine.

Next, Melisha hit record and dialed Jack's digits.

"Hey, babe," Jack said when he heard Melisha's voice. He had to quickly turn down his Barry White CD.

"Hi, honey bunny." Being nice to this prick was making Melisha sick. But she went through with her you're-still-my-man act. No matter what anyone said, Melisha knew she could put on a good performance. Anyway, she'd butter up this bonk-everybody boy as much as she needed to.

It was *all* for an excellent cause.

"I got it!" Melisha burst into Ellen's room holding a cassette tape in her hand. Meg was waving her arms around, trying uselessly to break up her smoke cloud.

"Is it juicy?" Meg asked, twirling her nose ring around with her forefinger and thumb. She was bummed because Ellen just told her how badly things had gone with Julian. Meg needed some good news — even if it came from Melisha the Monster.

"It's better than good. We're definitely having a party at my place on Friday. I mean a *big bash*," Melisha said.

That's when Ellen interrupted, "Look, I'm out — I'm sick of this bullshit." After what had happened with Julian, she didn't want anything to do with revenge on *anybody*.

"Oh no you don't, my main girlfriend," Meg said. Melisha kept quiet and hoped Meg could talk some sense into her. Melisha noticed that Meg had safety pins fastened in a row up the sides of her jeans.

"You're like Wiener-dog weird," Melisha commented to Meg.

"Shut up," Ellen and Meg replied in unison.

"Anyway, Ellen, you *are* in on this scheme with us," Meg said, noticing Melisha's tacky leopard-print tube top but opting to keep her mouth shut.

"Look, revenge isn't the answer to everything. I'm telling you — and I'm the one who knows," Ellen said.

"Don't let a little bad blood with Julian get you down. Jack actually *deserves* what he's getting," Meg added.

"*Julian?* Oh my, I *have* been out of the loop lately," Melisha said. "Anyway, don't you remember what Jack did to you? One of the last times I was in this bedroom, you were making a plan to humpty-dumpty him. Then —"

"Yeah, tell me what happened then, Melisha," Ellen said sarcastically. "Bitch," she added, under her breath.

"Well, whatever. You just have to get him back with us, honey," Melisha said. "When we get through with him, that boy will be Kal-Kan."

Inspired, Ellen answered, "Yeah, I guess so. I can't let you two have all the glory." She was rock-bottom down about Julian kicking her curbside — but this get-Jack plan was slowly revving her up. He was not a nice dude. It was about time he learned that he couldn't go around toying with girls. From now on, he would have to suffer the consequences. Hopefully he'd think twice about his player ways when they were through with him.

"So, my house, my party, our night. Don't forget! Tell *everyone at school* — I won't be there this week. I gotta run, girls. Toodles!" Melisha popped out the door.

"Ugggh," Meg said when she left.

"I know, major annoying, huh? At least she's got the goods."

CHAPTER TWENTY-TWO

Melisha hummed a tune from *Rent* while she put up a bunch of pony-print streamers. She even bought a strobe light and some Lava lamps on the el cheapo at the Goodwill. Not only was this going to be the event of the semester, she was also going to reclaim her rightful place on the local cool-o-meter.

Not to mention the fact that Melisha would help ensure that Jack had his rightful place in Shitville High infamy. No boy played her without learning his lesson. And when Jack started pulling the same old crap on her, well, he didn't realize that she wasn't Ellen, who sat back for so long. Melisha was aware that she had a mean streak, one that wasn't about to be wasted. Jack would soon be history.

Ellen and Meg arrived early to help set up. They brought the keg of Rolling Rock that Pearl had bought for them. Melisha's mom had promised to be gone for the evening, which made underage drinking a lot easier. Plus, the two girls brought the livest tunes around.

Ellen dumped out her CDs, then said: "If we left the music to Melisha, we'd have to listen to *Phantom of the Opera* all night."

"Well, I'm not listening to that creepy Coma Barfing Spaghettis shit," Melisha said.

"You wouldn't know cool if it smacked you," Meg said to Melisha.

"Oh, excuse me, nose-ring infection."

"Shut up, Pretty in Pink."

"I had Eve tell everyone to show up around seven. She spoke to every social Shitville butterfly," Ellen interrupted.

"I told Jack to show up around nine," Melisha added.

"We'll sneak in your back door at nine-o-five," Meg said.

The party was raging when Meg and Ellen pulled up in the pink Pinto. They could hear the Biggie music going bam, bam, bam.

Meg was *not* looking forward to her first non-Coma party. "If this is as lame as I think it's gonna be, I'm outtie by nine-thirty."

"Oh, it'll be lame," Ellen said.

They walked in the door and headed downstairs to join the party. Everyone stared at Meg because her hair was the same color as her car. They stared at Ellen because supposedly she and Melisha hated each other. But as soon as Melisha came hopping up to talk to Ellen, most people went back to drinking.

Meg seemed horrified to see football team boys smashing Bud beer cans on their foreheads. They dared a drunk freshman girl to try it — she did, and fell backward on the floor — out cold. Meg stepped over her and headed to Melisha's old toy room, where the stereo was booming. She and Ellen went outside for some air.

"These people are like *Animal House*," Meg said.

"Yeah, only worse. Imagine *Animal House* with zero IQs and

130

on acid. That's about as close as you'll get to any real conversation."

Meg agreed and passed Ellen a cigarette. Then they rushed inside because it was about five till nine. They took their places crouched next to the tape player. They didn't want Jack to see them when he walked in.

Meanwhile, the crowd was growing. Drunk cheerleaders were gettin' down to the song "Scrubs." One was doing a free erotic dance while the football team cheered her on. A few others were making out on the dance floor.

Then Jack made his entrance. Everyone grabbed, hugged, and kissed him as he bounced to the beat of the music. He was smiling and brushing his hands against all the girls' butts. To Jack, his slick, I'm-all-that image was *e-v-e-r-y-t-h-i-n-g*.

"He's an insult to all mankind, especially the female of the species," Meg commented.

"He's a puke."

Jack didn't notice them. Instead he kissed Melisha deeply — puttin' on a show for the benefit of all his pals, who, of course, clapped. Then Jack went to the keg, took a few gulps straight from the tap, and hit the dance floor.

He was gettin' down when the song mixed into a guy's voice.

Everyone stopped dancing and started laughing. The voice was Jack's — the party pack just thought it was a cool, Jack-like joke. But it was much more complicated than that.

Jack's voice blared over the stereo, saying: "Yeah, I know my buddy Bump is kinda cool, but he's a f-ing fat-ass who can't play football."

Now everyone went silent. The only sound in the room was Bump's growling. Jack's voice kept right on going — Melisha had been smart to edit out her own part of this setting-him-up phone conversation. "You used to like Brandon? Ewwww! I've seen him in the locker room. That boy's got a Twizzler weenie. And, yeah, Luke thinks me and him are cool, but I think he's the biggest loser. He can't even afford McDonald's — that's why he goes to White Castle."

Ellen, Meg, and Melisha were grinnin' large.

The tape went on and on. Melisha had gotten Jack to trash every homecoming-queen-crowd member at Shitville. At once, Jack rushed over to the stereo. Meg stood right in front of it — daring him to lay one finger on her five-foot body. She was holding her brass knuckles up to his face. Then, from behind, Bump tackled Jack to the ground, punching him and yelling, "Who you calling fat-ass, dickhead?" Brandon and Luke jumped Jack next. During the chaos, Ellen and Meg slipped out the door. Melisha was cackling with delight.

Jack wriggled his way off the floor and started sprinting up the stairway. Angry partyers reached out to slap Jack as he pushed his way through the crowd and out the front door.

"I totally lied about meeting your mother," Meg said as he ran past her. "I just wondered if you'd ever talk to a Coma, even if you had a good reason to. You didn't. You proved my point. You are one selfish, self-absorbed lughead."

"You did what?" Jack said. "You did not do that to me!!!"

He went around his car fishing frantically for his keys. He found them but couldn't get in his Beetle — Ellen was standing against the driver's-side door.

"Go to hell, Ellen," Jack said.

"I've already gone out with you," she replied as she moved out of his way. He sat down in his black Beetle and started the

132

engine. He looked up. Someone had written *LOSER* on his windshield in soap. His hood was covered in smashed eggs. He started cussing, then shifted into first gear. But he couldn't go anywhere.

Eve was standing on the other side of the car with a pocketknife in her hand. She knew about their plot. It's not like they were quiet about it.

"That is for my sister," she yelled to him, then turned around and went back to the party. With four slashed tires, Jack wasn't going anywhere. He jumped out of the car and ran down the street. A pack of football players were hot on his tail.

Ellen and Meg gave each other five. "Nice work, girlfriend!" Meg yelled.

"Can you believe Eve, though? That was cool as hell. I wish we would have thought of Eve's little trick ourselves!" Ellen added.

Their work was obviously done — Ellen and Meg hopped in the Pinto and drove away.

CHAPTER TWENTY-THREE

If they could have driven off into the sunset in a '67 Chevy convertible, Ellen and Meg still wouldn't have felt cooler.

But instead, they drove into the darkness of Melisha's suburban street and rolled down the Pinto windows. They headed to the nearby falls of the Ohio River. Most people went there to make out, but it was also a great place to sit and talk and ponder life. Meg pulled up to the edge of the water, then stopped the car. She put in an Ani DiFranco tape and got out of the car. Ellen followed her. They both sat on the hood sharing Gobstoppers.

"You know what?" Ellen said, finally breaking the silence. "This has been a really rough semester for me."

"Every semester is unbearable. I can't wait to go to college. The only thing I'll miss is you . . . and maybe Pearl."

"You know, you've been really cool to me. I just want to tell you that. I mean, my whole world turned upside down."

"Oh, I just helped you turn it right side up again, that's all," Meg said.

"Yeah, that's what you did."

"Ellen?" Meg asked, lying back on the hood, looking at the

stars. "Have you ever seen a horror flick called *Devil Dogs, Hounds of Hell?*"

Ellen laughed.

"I'm serious."

"No," Ellen said.

"Well, there is this really cute pack of puppies in the beginning. Then they grow up to be flesh-chewing beasts who get revenge on every person who's ever mistreated an animal."

"And you're telling me this because?"

"Because . . . the dogs finally give up biting and chasing people because they want to be nice and get petted and eat Purina all the time. They become, like, *normal* house dogs."

Meg wasn't exactly a pro at opening up, but Ellen got the gist of what she was trying to say. "I'm already thinking of retiring from the revenge business," Ellen replied.

"Good, girlfriend — 'cause all this thinkin' is wearin' my ass out."

It was taking its toll on Ellen, too. She wasn't used to getting evil, then getting even. After all, Ellen had to wait until she hurt inside out before she was motivated to stop being stomped on and do some stomping herself. Not taking everyone's crap elevated her personal worth. Her actions proved their purpose — Ellen was not someone to be messed with. But that didn't mean she could be such a bad-ass for the rest of her life. First of all, it was exhausting. Second, it just wasn't her. Sure, she might give people a taste of their own medicine in the future. But for now, she felt good and she was finished — except for one thing. . . .

"We haven't accomplished *everything* just yet," Ellen added.

"Oh no . . ."

"This one's easier, though."

"Oooooh, I get it. . . ."

"Julian," they both said.

Meg drove Ellen past his house. Meg was pressing Ellen to go knock on his door. But she refused — his Camry wasn't there.

"He's probably at Melisha's party," Meg said.

"Nah, he wouldn't go to a sleazefest like that. Maybe he's out with a girl or something."

"Now don't go jumpin' to conclusions. I can't handle going after some new bitch who's hangin' out with your man."

"He's not my man — I just wish we were friends again. You'd really like him, you know. Anyway, I'll try to talk to him later. Let's go home."

"We'll work on that tomorrow."

Ellen was ready to RIP by the time she arrived at the Hopkins house. She laid down in bed feeling exhausted but calmer than she had in months. She wasn't thinking of Jack or Melisha or even Eve. Her mind wasn't cluttered with schemes or plans or kicking ass.

But she *was* hungry.

She crawled out of bed to get a snack. Unfortunately, though, as she sat in the kitchen enjoying sweet chocolate bliss, Eve walked into the kitchen. She was obviously a little drunk.

"God, you smell like Wild Turkey," Ellen said.

"Save it. Look — I just did that tonight to show you —"

"Eve, you don't have to tell me anything."

"Just listen," she slurred. "I did it to show you that I don't hate you. I hope you don't hate me, either."

136

"Well, haven't you been reading my diary lately?" Ellen asked.

"No," Eve lied.

"If you had, you'd know that I felt bad about what happened to you with the teen program and all," Ellen explained. "They aren't going to air the tape, Eve. It's history."

"Oh, really? That's some good news."

"See, deep down, I don't hate you, either."

"But if you ever come into my room in the middle of the night again, I'll hit you harder."

"I promise to stay out of your room," Ellen said. *And your makeup box and Pantene bottle.* As far as Ellen was concerned, she and Eve were even. She vowed not to terrorize her sister again — well, as long as Eve didn't terrorize her.

Eve grabbed a bag of rice cakes on her way out of the room. Then she stopped and looked at Ellen all glassy-eyed. "You know, you're a weirdo just like Julian. He broke up with me. You knew that, right?"

"I guess I knew."

"Well, don't think I'm sweating him, sister. I'm already working on a new man. Julian is all yours."

"Like I need *your* permission."

Eve's eyes got squinty and she walked closer to Ellen. Eve propped herself up on a kitchen chair.

"I'm not giving you *permission*, Ellen. I'm just saying that if you ever plan to get another boyfriend, Julian's the one for you."

Then she stumbled up the stairs — leaving Ellen alone with her thoughts.

CHAPTER TWENTY-FOUR

Julian was in the middle of a great dream. He was Brad Pitt's character in *Thelma and Louise,* making out big-time with Thelma, whose face looked just like —

Then his phone rang, ruining the whole thing. It was just like when you see part of the movie, and then it's due back to the video store before you get to finish it. Julian was tired of disappointment. As he shook his grogginess, he looked at his watch. Why was the phone ringing? It was eight in the morning on a Sunday.

"Hello."

"Uh, hi," the girl on the other line said.

"Who is this?" Julian asked. At first listen, the voice made him think he was still dreaming. As he heard a few sniffs and a whimper, though, he knew he would never be quite that lucky.

"It's Eve," the girl said. She had kinda-sorta sounded like Ellen, but Ellen would never whine. Eve, on the other hand, never stopped.

"You sound weird. Have you been crying?" Still, he was concerned about her.

"My parents are in a huge fight. I can't deal."

"What happened? Are you okay?"

"No, I'm not. Will you meet me at Denny's in half an hour? I don't have anyone to talk to."

"Sure, I guess . . . I'll be right there."

Julian put on his clothes reluctantly — scared of what he was getting himself into with Eve. But being the good ex-boyfriend, he picked up the pace, quickly brushed his teeth, and left.

Ellen arrived at Denny's, worried that Meg was in some kind of trouble. When she got there, she thought she might be hallucinating — Julian was sitting alone at a booth. She walked toward his table, but he didn't see her.

"Hey," Ellen said.

Julian looked just as surprised to see her.

"Have you seen Meg?" Ellen asked.

"No, I'm actually looking for your sister. Was there a bad fight at your house this morning?"

"No, but Meg just called me crying and said *her* parents were in a great big fight."

They just stared at each other awkwardly.

"Julian, are you sure it was Eve who called you? She was sleeping when I left."

"Now that I think about it, she sounded weird. Do you think your friend Meg is up to something?"

"That's my guess."

"Well, sit down if you want to," Julian offered.

"No, maybe I should go."

"It's okay, sit down."

Ellen didn't really know what to say. She had everything and nothing to tell Julian. "Are you still furious about the college application thing?"

"Yeah."

"Would it help if I said I was sorry again?" Ellen asked.

"I don't know," he lied — anything she said definitely helped.

"Sorry." Ellen said. "Really, really sorry," she added. "Sorry some more," she added again.

He didn't say anything to her. Instead, he hid his relief at hearing her words. Julian was going to make her work for this one.

"Look, I'd really like us to be friends again. Do you think we could hang out during lunch together again sometime?"

Silence. Julian could sense her frustration. He liked to see her frustrated; it was cute.

"Um, what do you want me to do? Just tell me."

"Honestly, Ellen, I want you to cut out all the bullshit," Julian said. "Why do you keep bugging me?" *Keep bugging me, Ellen, keep bugging me,* his brain said to his insides.

At first Ellen was offended by the term "bugging." But she could figure out what Julian wanted — a straightforward monologue on how she felt about him. She knew him well enough to figure out that when he said he was tired of playing games, he meant it. That's when she started sweating; all of this fessing up emotionally wasn't exactly her strong suit. "I missed you this last month," she muttered.

He couldn't help it, he smiled a tiny bit. "Oh yeah?"

"I found out that it was really tough to be without you."

"Tell me more. . . ."

"Um, I was completely consumed by jealousy when you started seeing my sister."

"Okay." Julian was really enjoying this.

"Look," Ellen pleaded. "I didn't want to hurt you. I didn't meant to. I guess I . . . I mean I . . . I swear I didn't know what I was doing. I was so into this whole revenge thing that I turned into someone else. I was intoxicated by being mean to people who were mean to me. Then I totally lost my mind and was mean to you, too. You hadn't been cruel to me at all. It's just that you hurt me. You don't know it, but you really did. You didn't want anything to do with me, then you dated my sister. I did those things because they gave me some sort of sick power. But I don't want that anymore. I don't want people to be scared of me. I don't want to be the girl who's good at getting even. I just want to have the quiet, close relationships I used to have. I want that with you . . . I want more with you."

"So where does that leave us?"

"Do I have to keep going?" She would, but she didn't want to.

"Ellen, don't toy with me," he said. "I care about you. And I don't know if you feel the same way about me."

Ellen lifted herself off the booth and reached across the table. She kissed him gently and passionately. "Now do you know?" she asked. She couldn't believe she had just done that. It was just a natural, knee-jerk reaction.

Completely, pleasantly surprised at Ellen's display of affection, Julian plopped down his three dollars and got up to leave.

She looked at him, confused. She took this huge, gigantic, potentially mortifying step of kissing him, and he was getting up to leave? It felt like her lungs had processed their last bits of oxygen and closed up for good. Her muscles were tense all over. *Oh, don't make me suffer!*

He read her mind, grabbed her hand, and smiled. Her face and body finally went less tense — he could feel it because she stood so close to him. They walked out of Denny's together, stood at the car, and kissed again. He was going to show her what she'd been missing all of the time he'd been in love with her.

That, he decided, would be the sweetest revenge.

CUT *by Patricia McCormick*
KEROSENE *by Chris Wooding*
PURE SUNSHINE *by Brian James*
YOU REMIND ME OF YOU *by Eireann Corrigan*

IN STORES NOW